An inheritance of twenty [illegible] and a house in Grosvenor Street! Just what is badly needed by Lady Angel, the fond mama of three daughters about to be established in *ton* society. But the conduct of the eldest of her girls leaves a lot to be desired. Why does the delectable Prue show such stupid reluctance to encourage the handsome, rakish Duke of Carlington, when chance throws them together? The Duke is certainly known throughout Georgian London as the Perfidious Devil, and renowned for his *amours*, but why should a girl of Prue's beauty and spirit be so unwilling to take advantage of his obvious interest?

*By the same author in Masquerade*

RUNAWAY MAID

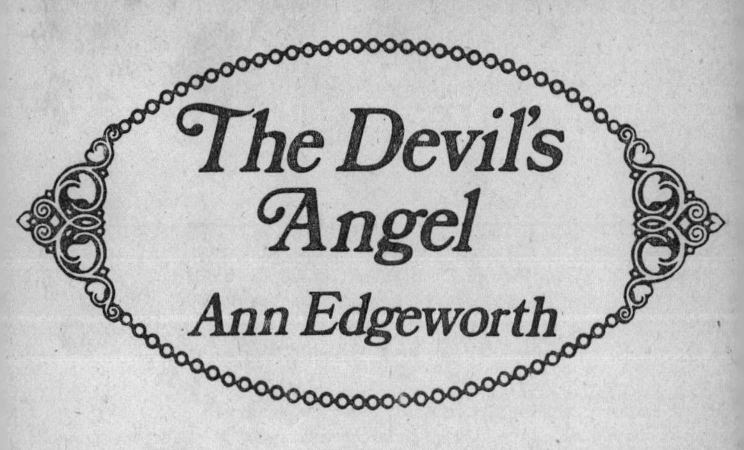

MILLS & BOON LIMITED
London · Sydney · Toronto

*First published in Great Britain 1980*
*by Mills & Boon Limited, 15–16 Brook's Mews,*
*London W1*



ISBN 0 263 73229 0



Set in Plantin 10 on 11½ pt

*Made and printed in Great Britain by*
*C. Nicholls & Company Ltd*
*The Philips Park Press, Manchester*

# CHAPTER ONE

'INDEED, sir, I find you vastly inconsiderate of your family,' Lady Angel said pettishly.

Sir Roland Angel looked up from his desk, keeping his quill pen in his hand as he replied,

'I do not agree, madam. I think I consider you very well. Country air and peaceful surroundings are a deal better than the dirt and foul vapours of London.'

'But you have daughters, sir,' his wife said, snapping her fan shut, 'three of them, growing into maidenhood all too fast.'

''Tis the way of young females, I believe,' her husband observed.

Lady Angel chose to ignore this. 'Are they to marry country bumpkins or wither into unwanted old maids, pray?'

'At least a country bumpkin will not plague his wife with mistresses or game away his inheritance,' Sir Roland said, bending to his writing again. 'Let me hear no more of this prattle of going to London and a society season for our daughters, madam. I have neither the mind nor fortune for it.'

His wife rustled her petticoats and pouted, but he paid no heed. After a few minutes had passed, she renewed her attack.

'All the girls have good looks, and they should be allowed a chance to make suitable marriages and not waste themselves on such callow youths as they meet here. I vow Selina is already too interested in that young Jim West, who is nothing but a rough creature with no genteel manners about him.'

The door opened softly and a pretty, golden-haired girl peeped in.

'Mama, can Cassie and I ride over to West House? Jim has a new mare——'

'No, miss, you may not! Jim has nothing but horses and hunting in his head,' her mother snapped. 'I do not wish you to see so much of him. That young man has ideas above his station. Where, pray, is your sister Prue?'

'She's taken the pony trap to the village to collect the post, Mama.'

'I trust the groom is with her?'

Selina giggled. 'Oh, that isn't Prue's way, she don't bother with grooms.'

'Then she shall be scolded! It is not seemly for a young girl to be driving about the country alone. What will neighbours think? It is high time Prue learned to behave.'

'Well, here she comes now,' Selina moved aside to allow a slim, dark-eyed girl in a blue pelisse and bonnet to enter. 'What comes in the post, sister?'

'Two for Papa and a most solemn-looking one for Mama,' Prue said, and gave a letter into her mother's outstretched hand.

'From London! Now who should be writing to me from London?' her mother murmured as she broke the seal and began to read. After some minutes she gave a small scream, causing both girls to turn and stare at her and Selina to ask eagerly,

'What is it, Mama? Is it of interest?'

''Twill be a pleasant change for something of interest to happen to us,' Prue declared, pulling off her bonnet and shaking her dark curls free. 'I vow this is the dullest house in the kingdom!'

Lady Angel's plump cheeks were scarlet and she appeared to be struggling for words. At last she managed to gasp out,

'Oh Sir Roland! Daughters! Such a shock! Such a splendid surprise! So extraordinary an answer to my prayer!'

Her husband looked up. 'And who, pray, answers your prayer in so convenient a fashion, madam?'

''Tis from my sister Fanny's lawyer, sir. Oh, I declare I am all of a twitter! I must beg a glass of wine! My heart. . . .' She laid a hand on the bodice of her chintz morning-gown. 'Poor Fanny is dead! Imagine it, and she five years younger than I!'

Prue poured out a glass of wine and gave it to her mother saying, 'Indeed it must be a shock for you, Mama. Poor Aunt Fanny! Pray compose yourself and tell us more of it.'

'A *splendid* surprise, I think you said?' her husband remarked, raising his eyebrows.

'Oh, I did not mean . . . Of course poor Fanny and I never did get along well, and she positively refused to invite us to London so that the girls could see something of the fashionable world. I cannot pretend I feel her death excessively. Of course it is very sad, but her life was not much since she became widowed and an invalid.'

Her eyes returned to the letter she still held. 'But I fear I have misjudged her over the years. How could I ever know she would remember me so generously! So vastly unexpected an inheritance! She must have repented of all her spiteful behaviour!'

'Mama!' Prue grabbed her mother's shoulders and shook her, not over-gently. '*Will* you tell us what is in the letter?'

'Restrain yourself, hoyden! I've a mind to tell you nothing.'

Prue snatched the letter and ran to the window, ignoring her mother's expostulations.

'Good God! She has left you her house in Grosvenor Street . . . and twenty thousand pounds! Mama! Papa!' She whirled about, her eyes ablaze with excitement. 'Does it mean we can go to London?'

Sir Roland glanced at his wife and shrugged. 'I very much

fear it does. Your mother is already planning your wardrobe for your entry into the modish world, no doubt.'

Selina ran to the door. 'Cassie! Come to us! Mama has received such a letter, and we are all overset! Pray hurry!'

Her twin sister came running. Both girls had golden curls and deeply blue eyes and charming dimples, but there was more character in Cassie's face and more assurance in her manner.

'What's the ferment?' she demanded. As her sisters proceeded to tell her, her eyes widened. 'A London house? Mama, now we can have a season in London! Routs, balls, parties, assemblies . . . perhaps be presented to His Majesty King George and Queen Charlotte!'

'No doubt it will be a fine occasion for their Majesties,' her father observed dryly.

'Though 'tis said the receptions are uncommonly drear,' Cassie went on, ignoring him, 'and the Queen vastly prim and proper. When can we set off, Mama?' She tugged at her mother's skirts. 'Can we have new gowns and——'

'Quiet, little wretch, my head is quite spinning.' Lady Angel sipped her wine and lay back in her chair. 'No doubt there will be much business to be seen to before we get house or money. But once all is settled. . . .'

'You will proceed to take the capital by storm,' Sir Roland said, rising. 'I fear you must go alone, madam. I have no intention of accompanying you on this rash venture. You know no one of note in London, no one who will sponsor the girls.'

'Indeed I do, husband! Dorcas Beauford is in town and has always shown me the greatest friendship, and has often remarked how unfortunately our daughters are placed, being so far from good society. There is no truly genteel society in Northumberland. Dorcas has two daughters who are debutantes this year; such extraordinarily plain girls, poor things.'

'She may not show us much favour if we appear in London and make comparison with her daughters,' Prue remarked shrewdly.

'I wash my hands of the affair,' Sir Roland said curtly. 'I am too old to enjoy the so-called delights of society, and my health will not allow my living in a city. Make what you like of your inheritance, madam, but pray leave me in peace.'

'Such an unnatural husband and father,' Lady Angel lamented when he had gone, 'to let us go alone to London. Mark my words, it will be remarked upon.'

'We shall spread it around that he is an invalid and must remain in Northumberland,' Prue said. She drew a deep breath and clasped her hands. 'Surely it is a gift from the gods! A season in London! And husbands for us all—wealthy, titled husbands!'

'Prue, 'tis unbecoming for you to say so,' her mother said in a shocked voice.

'I say what we are all thinking. *I* do not wish to marry a gentleman-farmer or small squire. I am tired of being buried in Northumberland. I long to see London, to enter society and have pretty gowns and handsome admirers, and dance and—and *live*!' She flung her arms wide, her dark eyes dancing. 'And when I tire of it all, I shall find a husband with a fine fortune and—yes—a title!'

Her mother rose from her chair. 'You talk in a most unmaidenly way which ill fits you to be the wife of any man, let alone a man of fashion. I must get your father to attend to the business of this letter, and discover how soon we may move into Grosvenor Street. Such a great event! Such a splendid change of fortune for us all! Quite sad about poor Fanny, of course.'

'I think I never met her,' Prue said thoughtfully, 'but I shall ever be grateful to her. However, would it not be more honest to admit we cannot feel *excessive* sorrow at her death?'

'Prue!' Lady Angel flung up her hands in dismay. 'Such

unfeeling words! I have a mind to leave you behind when we go to London.'

'To marry a gentleman-farmer who thinks of nothing but his cows and pigs?' Prue dropped a light kiss on her mother's cheek. 'No, Mama, you shall take me with you. No doubt but London will teach me genteel manners.'

Sir Roland's estate was small. His father had been ruined by unwise speculation and had left little fortune. Sir Roland was a studious man of simple tastes who had no sympathy with his wife's social ambitions; but to bring peace, he took the matter of the inheritance in hand and wrote to the lawyers. The settlement of affairs took longer than Lady Angel had hoped, and it was late spring before plans could be made for residence in Grosvenor Street. A fine bustle of preparation then ensued, from which Sir Roland absented himself, shutting himself up in his library and declaring he had done his part.

The twins took after their mother in their pink-and-white beauty, but Prue had her father's fine, expressive dark eyes and thick, glossy hair. She had a quick and lively mind, and a firmness of character and quick temper her mother deplored. Like her sisters, she was enchanted with the prospect of entering the social life of the capital and took the trouble to bully the village dressmaker into making her two simple gowns for her to wear until her mother's friend, Mrs Beauford, could put her in touch with a fashionable establishment in London.

'How I long to attend the theatre,' Selina sighed, tossing aside the *London Gazette*. 'And drive in the park, and visit Vauxhall and—and——'

'And find yourself a rich husband,' Prue added, bending over the bonnet she was trimming. 'Mama will be disappointed unless you catch a Marquis, or at least an Honourable.'

'Oh I'm determined to make a good match,' Selina said,

'I've no mind to live in a dismal house like this.' She looked around her at the big, ill-lit room with its shabby furniture and tall windows looking out on to lawns and woods swept by brisk spring winds.

It was an ugly, inconvenient house, but Prue had a fondness for it. She had been born and spent a happy childhood in it, and had not felt the need of a wider life until she had grown to girlhood. Now, her restless spirit chafed against the lack of congenial neighbours, the distance from any town of consequence and the bleak countryside around her. To exchange all this for the delights of a city could mean nothing but purest bliss! She was swept with excitement whenever she thought of what could lie ahead for her.

Cassie, who was half-heartedly trying to mend a tear in some lace, asked idly, 'Prue, would you marry your wealthy nobleman if you did not love him?'

Prue considered, her head on one side and needle poised.

'No. A loveless marriage would not be a successful one. I intend to find someone I *can* love and respect, then all will be well.'

'But suppose we don't meet any suitable gentlemen?' Selina asked uneasily. 'Mrs Beauford may refuse to introduce us into society as she has daughters of her own wanting husbands.'

'Then we shall promenade the parks with placards!' Prue declared, springing up, her dark eyes dancing, 'saying "Wanted immediately, three wealthy gentlemen of noble birth. Apply between ten and noon at Twenty-two, Grosvenor Street!"' She began to march up and down the room waving her bonnet, while her sisters dissolved into laughter.

Lady Angel entered the room and shook her head. 'Fie, you behave like a pack of schoolchildren! And it is you, Prue, as ever, who leads you into nonsense. I have news for you; we have heard we may remove to Grosvenor Street as soon as we choose. *Prue*!' She endeavoured to disentangle herself from Prue's encircling arms. 'Pray have done! You are upsetting my cap!'

'Oh, Mama, are we truly going at last?' Prue released her mother and danced to the window. 'No more grass and trees! We shall look out on London streets with coaches, crowds, horsemen. . . . Oh! I can barely wait!'

'If you are so impatient, you can help Lizzie plan my packing,' her mother told her. ''Tis never too early to start, and she is sadly stupid at folding my gowns. See to it, child.'

The house was thrown into turmoil, with Lady Angel giving the staff contradictory orders and changing her mind a dozen times a day. She wrote to her dear friend, Mrs. Beauford, who answered effusively and with assurances of being able and willing to introduce them all into the most genteel society, and promised to call upon them as soon as they were settled in their new home.

Alone in her bedroom, Prue gave some serious thought to the future.

'The twins must marry well. It will not be a problem, they are beauties even if they are feather-heads. But *I* shall have to work harder, for I'm no beauty, I fear me.'

She turned to her looking-glass and regarded herself critically. A slim, graceful figure, fresh complexion, dark curling hair and great soft dark eyes that were her best feature. Pretty, yes, she told herself, but nothing exceptional.

'Luckily I gave more heed to my schooling and have a quicker mind than my sisters,' she thought.

She invaded her father's solitude one morning to ask a question that had been troubling her.

'Dear Papa, are you not to enjoy part of our aunt's bequest?'

He shook his head. 'I have no need of, or desire for, a

penny of it. I have all I desire, and I shall have a fine period of tranquillity when you are all gone to the city.' He smiled at her, his favourite daughter. 'The twins chatter all day like starlings. But I shall miss you, Prue. I sometimes wonder if I am right to allow your mother to thrust you into the world of fashion.'

'Why, sir, 'tis what we have been dreaming of this long while. You must know that London with its modish delights and fine company seems paradise to us.'

'To you it may seem so,' he sighed. 'To one who knows what plots are hatched, what shallow aims are pursued there, it is far from any paradise. I do not care for present-day politics. Lord North may be a good man, but he is not strong enough to oppose the King's wishes, and I see danger ahead for the country and trouble with our American colonies. And in Parliament factions fight, not for England's glory, but for selfish ends.'

'Oh, for sure,' Prue agreed sunnily, 'but dear Papa, we do not go to London intending to reform Parliament.'

At last the day for departure drew near. The big travelling chaise was to take Lady Angel, her daughters and Lizzie, Lady Angel's abigail, and a smaller coach the luggage and three servants. Bags and trunks were packed and corded and bandboxes strapped, and rugs and cushions piled in the chaise for greater comfort in travelling.

A morning was spent bidding farewell to neighbours, and later Prue found Selina mopping her eyes in a corner and asked the reason.

''Tis poor Jim. He says he'll never forget me, but for sure I will forget *him* and it will break his heart! 'Tis most affecting, is it not?'

'Well, I confess I think it extremely likely,' Prue said frankly. 'You won't hold him long in your thoughts once you reach London.'

'Why 'tis likely I shan't,' Selina agreed, brightening up. 'I shall find plenty of handsome blades to flirt with there, I warrant you.'

On the night before their departure, Sir Roland sent for Prue. She found him in the library, standing beside the window. He turned as she entered.

'I desire to speak to you before you leave, child. I know you are as set on this venture as your mother and sisters, and I cannot prevent your going to London.'

'Indeed you could, sir, by ordering me to remain here.'

He waved his hand impatiently. 'And have you railing at me every minute? No, you must go. But it is my duty as your father to warn you that you may be going into danger, danger that your mother cannot, or will not, acknowledge. I have no fear for your sisters, they are pretty noddle-heads, but you are different.' He looked at her as she stood before him, slight and graceful in her striped morning gown. 'You have always been high-spirited; your mother has been lax in her discipline.'

'And you, sir, have never disciplined me at all,' Prue reminded him, smiling mischievously.

He sighed. 'I fear 'tis true. But I am a tired man and my health is frail.' He was silent for a time, his head bent. Then he straightened up. 'You know little of the world, of its evil, its false promises—and you know nothing of men, and there lies your greatest danger. You will meet many men, few of whom you can trust. You are not a great beauty, but you have some quality, a vital spark, that will draw men to you. I tremble for you, Prue.'

She ran to him, her eyes soft. 'I promise to be careful. My one regret is leaving you. Could you not come with us?'

He shook his head. 'I am a selfish man; perhaps I should not have had children.' He took her hand. 'But I would not wish to be without you, Prue, and I am troubled for you.'

'Do not fear,' she begged. 'I am your daughter, I shall not forget I am an Angel.'

His smile was wry. 'In faith, I sometimes think there is a spice of the devil in you as well, child.' He sank into a chair. 'Go now, and try to remember what I have told you.'

The sun was rising in glory, painting the sky rose and gold, when the two coaches lumbered down the drive next morning. Lady Angel was irritable and fussy from having to rise so early and the twins were whispering together. Prue was quiet, aware of a strange feather-touch of fear. What if her father was right and she was entering a world where she would find danger and perhaps heartbreak? It was true she knew nothing of men. Such as she had met had been sons of impoverished families whose parents had been unwilling, or unable, to educate them at university or allow them to mingle with the fashionable world.

For a second, her slender fingers tightened on the little reticule she carried; then her courage returned and she raised her chin defiantly. She would be able to look after herself. She would soon learn where danger lay and how to avoid it. To go to London had always been her dream, and now her dream was coming true!

# CHAPTER TWO

THE roads were in bad condition. Spring rains had pitted the ill-kept highways and made quagmires of the lower levels, and travelling was slow and uncomfortable. The inns at which the party had put up had been poor and the food coarse, and now, as the heavy chaise rumbled along a country road with rain-filled ditches on either side, Lady Angel sighed peevishly and sought her vinaigrette.

'I trust you remembered to bring the Peruvian Bark, Lizzie? Such ill weather and rough travel well may produce fevers. I shall need at least a week's rest to recover from this vile journey.'

'Thank heaven we should be in London tonight,' Prue said. 'Perhaps the roads may improve as we approach the city.'

As she spoke, she heard a shout and the jingle of harness as the horses were pulled up, and letting down the window, she put her head out and saw a man in a stained coat speaking to Lawson, the coachman.

'What is it?' her mother demanded in a flutter. 'Oh, heaven! Is it a highwayman? Prue! Cassie! Selina! Say we are poor females with no jewels or——'

'Peace, Mama,' Prue withdrew her head, ''tis a man who has met with an accident and asks our help.'

The light, elegant landau lay tipped in a ditch, its hood half wrenched off and one wheel in the air. Two trembling horses stood on one side, their cut harness dangling, and a tall man in a mud-splashed greatcoat was sitting on a bank nursing an arm.

A groom appeared at the coach window to explain. The landau had tried to avoid a pothole and had landed in the ditch, and the gentleman on the bank had hurt his arm and was in need of a surgeon.

'His Grace would be grateful if you could carry him to the next town, ma'am,' the groom bobbed his head deferentially to Lady Angel. ''Tis but a mile off.'

'His Grace?' Lady Angel gasped.

'Yes, ma'am, 'tis his Grace the Duke of Carlington, and his arm is uncommon painful to him.'

Lady Angel, quite overcome, managed to say faintly, 'I shall be pleased to render my lord Duke all assistance necessary.'

The gentleman had risen, wincing somewhat, and now approached the chaise and bowed. He was tall and broad of shoulder, and his thick chestnut hair was unpowdered. His fine tricorne hat floated in a nearby ditch.

'I am vastly obliged to you, madam. I regret the accident which has brought me to this pass and made it necessary to ask your aid.' He looked up and Prue met a pair of cool grey eyes that surveyed her speculatively before returning to Lady Angel, upon whose face had appeared a gracious simper. 'If I may beg a seat beside your coachman——'

'La, Your Grace, 'twill not do, there is rain coming,' Lady Angel protested. 'You must come inside. Lizzie, go sit outside and make way for His Grace, a trifle of rain will not hurt you.'

The gentleman's protests, as a sulky Lizzie got out of the chaise, were somewhat half-hearted. His eyes returned to Prue, who pretended not to notice, although she felt her heart quicken a trifle. He gave some instructions to his groom about the horses, then entered the chaise and sat down with a grimace of pain.

'I fear I am not in a condition to sit with ladies,' he

apologised, 'I am sadly mud-stained.'

'Oh 'tis the smallest matter, Your Grace,' Lady Angel assured him. 'How is your arm, is it broken?'

'No, but I confess it is not very comfortable.'

'Is there anything we may do for it? I have a medicine chest with me.'

'Thank you, no, madam. 'Twill be best to consult a surgeon. May I tender my grateful thanks for your assistance?'

His words were respectful, but Prue saw how boldly his eyes roved over them, and she felt herself stiffen.

'May I be allowed to know the name of my good Samaritan?' he asked, smiling.

Lady Angel, her self-confidence returned, leaned forward eagerly.

'We are only too pleased to be of help, my lord Duke, I do assure you. I am Lady Angel, and these are my three daughters. We travel from Northumberland, a sadly long and uncomfortable journey.'

'Yes indeed, the highways are in a shocking state,' he said sympathetically. 'Are you to take up residence in London?'

He spoke to Lady Angel, but his eyes went to Prue, who instantly lowered hers. He was a very fine gentleman, and a Duke to boot, but his manner displeased her. The twins, wide-eyed, were in a flutter of excitement.

In a short time he had everything from Lady Angel. Prue tried to catch her mother's eye in warning, but the exhilaration of being in the company of a Duke—hopefully unmarried—drove caution to the winds.

'So you have a friend who will introduce you into society?' he said.

Lady Angel nodded complacently. 'Yes, a Mistress Beauford, a lady of good family with two sadly plain daughters.'

'Indeed, a most expedient acquaintance.' His tone was sympathetic, but Prue caught the flash of ironic amusement in his eyes and she bit her lip. 'May I be allowed the pleasure of calling upon you, Lady Angel, to tender my grateful thanks once more?'

'Oh, most certainly, my lord Duke! We shall be *honoured*! Such gracious condescension.... I'm sure we've done nothing....' Lady Angel subsided, speechless, in a flutter of awe and delight.

The Duke turned to Prue. She met his gaze coolly as he asked, 'Does the prospect of London gaieties please you, ma'am?'

She raised her slender brows slightly. 'I shall not know, Your Grace, until I have sampled them.'

He bent closer. 'But you are disposed to like them?'

'I am not disposed to like anything or anyone——' she laid a light emphasis on the last word, '——until I have proved them worthy of my liking.'

He let his eyes travel over her slowly. She was wearing a dark green braided pelisse, and a light lace scarf covered her dark curls. Her cheeks were delicately flushed and her eyes very bright.

He murmured, under cover of the rattle of wheels and creaking harness, 'May I be allowed to share some of the pleasures of London with you, Mistress Angel? It is possible I could open some doors for you and your family that might otherwise be unkindly closed to newcomers from the country. That is, if you would consent to be . . . a little kind to me.'

Prue sat up, stung by the veiled insolence of his words. Her dark eyes were suddenly full of fire and her lip curled as she said in a low, scornful voice, 'Thank you, Your Grace, but we have no need of your patronage! We have friends in London who will not require any particular . . . *kindness* in return for their attentions!'

He leant back against the upholstery of the carriage, smiling.

''Pon honour, may I suggest that your name may not be totally in accord with your nature, Mistress Angel?'

Prue turned abruptly and stared out of the window, but she remained most uncomfortably aware of his eyes assessing her with lazy interest which both displeased and disturbed her. He was handsome, but she did not admire him. He was noble, but she felt no reverence. He noticed her, but she was not gratified. He was attractive in his lazy arrogance, but she was not attracted. And yet she had felt her pulse flutter when his eyes met hers, and she was breathing unevenly as she studiously kept her head averted.

They came to a market town where their noble guest alighted, after thanking Lady Angel and repeating his intention of calling upon her in London. He had grown silent on the last part of the journey and Prue, glancing at him from under her long, dark lashes, saw how white and strained he looked, and guessed he was in pain from his injured arm.

She was relieved when he left them. That he was a rake she was fairly certain, and she regretted her mother's obsequious attentions to him. He was not a man to be encouraged, and her family would gain small esteem by his favours, and possibly lose it entirely if he chose to mark them out with especial notice. Already Cassie and Selina could talk of nothing but the Duke's charm, handsome looks and condescension, and her mother, she suspected, was contemplating the glory of having a Duke for a son-in-law, choosing to ignore the obvious truth that a man of such high rank would marry someone of equal birth, and that marriage was far from the thoughts of such as he, until he had tired of the delights of profligacy.

Her woman's instinct told her he was interested in her, that a pretty face and a piquant situation had aroused his jaded appetite for a moment. That he affected her in some strange and disturbing manner was unfortunate, but not disastrous. She would avoid him if he called—and it was more than possible he did not mean to—and would soon forget him in the excitement of London life. She would make her mother see that such a man as the Duke of Carlington could spell danger for them, although it might not be easy to wean her from her rosy dreams of the future.

Darkening skies and a steady drizzle of rain dampened all their spirits as they drew into the suburbs of the city and even the twins grew silent. Lady Angel dropped asleep in her corner as the coachman wove his way through thickening traffic.

'A somewhat shabby start,' Prue thought, wrapping herself in her pelisse and sinking back among her cushions, 'pray heaven things may improve before I am quite out of patience with London!'

Where was the expected thrill, the rapture at the fulfilment of her dearest wishes? Was it because, try as she would, she could not dismiss the memory of a pair of coolly amused grey eyes that had looked so deeply and disturbingly into hers?

# CHAPTER THREE

AUNT FANNY'S house was a disappointment. It was tall and narrow with long windows heavily draped and a hall made bleak by its black and white marble floor and dark panelling. The long drawing-room on the first floor had something of the same oppressive air with its dark hangings and heavy furniture, and as she entered it Prue could not help exclaiming, 'My poor aunt must have been of gloomy cast of mind! Why, 'tis more a mausoleum than a house!'

Cassie agreed. 'Mama, you must tear those curtains down and remove that dreary carpet. And that bronze statue is perfectly hideous!'

'Tush, child,' her mother rebuked her, 'it is a fine representation of . . . of . . .'

'Of poor Aunt Fanny's bad taste,' Prue said, tossing off her pelisse. 'Come, let us see if our bedrooms are as gloomy.'

The rooms above were sparsely furnished, as if Aunt Fanny had not thought them worthy of attention. Prue chose a small room looking out on to the street as being possible of improvement once she could persuade her mother to refurnish it.

Mrs Beauford, on Lady Angel's writing to request it, had engaged a staff, and a meal was ready by the time the weary travellers had changed their clothes. Tired as she was, Prue lay awake for some time that night, listening to the night sounds of the great city that were so different from the deep country quiet, that was only occasionally broken by the bark of a fox or an owl's plaintive cry, and trying to realise that she was at last in London.

For two weeks they were busy bringing some element of comfort and cheerfulness into Aunt Fanny's house. Then there were gowns to be ordered, together with bonnets and shoes, fans and reticules, ribbons and laces.

Cassie and Selina delighted in shopping and driving in the park with their mother, and strolling wherever they could feast their eyes on the world of fashion. Prue enjoyed such events also, but she occasionally slipped away with Lizzie or a footman in attendance to visit the Royal Academy, Westminster Abbey and some of the fine buildings she had read about. London, she decided, was truly interesting and very pleasant, and what she saw of the modish world of satins and brocades and jewels, fluttering fans and elegant bows and curtseys, gossip and snobbery diverted and amused her.

Mrs Beauford had made her appearance a few days after their arrival. She drove up in a smart equipage and rustled into the drawing-room to embrace her dearest friend and cast a startled and displeased eye on the daughters of the house.

'La! You've three fine bucolic girls, Clarissa,' she exclaimed, raising her quizzing-glass to stare through it at the girls. ''Tis not modish, you know, to be so plump and red-cheeked. You must condition them, my sweet Clarissa.'

'Like cattle for a cattle-show?' Prue asked demurely, and saw the lady bristle. She had taken a dislike to Mrs Beauford and had a strong suspicion she would like her daughters even less.

'Your country manners, young lady, will not do for polite society,' Mrs Beauford snapped. 'Such forwardness is vastly improper. His Majesty himself has been known to remark upon the free ways of some modern misses. I am lucky in having two daughters whose manners and elegant deportment have brought them nothing but approbation.'

'Indeed I am persuaded they are very fine young ladies,' Lady Angel agreed. 'My girls can hardly wait to meet them. We know few people in society as yet.' She smiled, the light of triumph in her eyes. 'But we have had a great honour, and in the strangest manner,' and she proceeded to tell of their adventures, stressing the Duke's interest in them and his expressed intention of renewing the acquaintanceship.

Mrs Beauford snapped her quizzing-glass shut. 'Indeed? Well, Clarissa, I feel it my duty to make you aware of His Grace's reputation! He is a sad libertine. There is little scandal that does not include his name.' She accepted a cup of tea and glanced at her friend. 'I would not let one of my dear girls so much as be seen walking with him.'

'Well, perhaps they won't get the chance to,' Cassie said guilelessly.

Mrs Beauford glared. 'No woman of reputation would have anything to do with him! You will be wise to close your door to him, Clarissa, if you value your daughters' virtue!'

'I have every regard for my daughters' virtue,' Lady Angel eyed her dearest friend with some asperity. 'The Duke behaved with the greatest respect to us. I have no doubt his reputation has been grossly blown up by persons who have *not* been honoured by his attentions.'

Prue left the ladies to their battle. She wished to hear no more of the man who lingered so vividly in her thoughts. *If* he should call—and she was sure he had never meant to—she would take care not to be present.

The Misses Beauford, Caro and Minnie, came a few days later. They were tall, thin, sandy-haired girls modishly dressed and with high voices and affected manners that made Prue smile and the twins stare.

'Oh, la! How I envy you seeing London for the first time!' Caro trilled, sinking into a chair and fanning herself. 'After being obliged to exist in the country! You must all be perfectly overset with such splendour!'

'Such a vast *change*,' Minnie agreed, blinking her pale lashes, 'to have to learn the ways of polite society.'

'Pray do not distress yourself,' Prue said calmly, 'politeness is not unknown in the country.'

'And we have society there too,' Cassie added. 'London is all very fine, no doubt, 'tis a pity there is so much dirt on the roads and so many poor wretches who must beg or steal if they are not to starve.'

'But we find the shops vastly interesting,' Selina broke in eagerly. 'Pray tell us what establishments you patronise.'

When the Beauford ladies had gone, the three girls looked at each other.

'Affected, noddle-headed little geese,' Prue declared.

'They were determined to put us down,' Cassie complained.

'But they were *excessively* fashionable,' Selina sighed. 'Miss Minnie has told me where I can buy a sweet shawl.'

Mrs Beauford, having promised an introduction into polite society, could hardly withdraw the offer on having discovered her dearest friend's daughters to be so dismayingly attractive. The Angel family met some of the Beaufords' acquaintances and people began to call on them, and soon the girls had made friends with other young females with whom to gossip, compare fashions and attend small, genteel gatherings. It was early in the season and His Majesty, King George, was still at Weymouth.

One sunny afternoon the family was sitting in the drawing-room, which had been much improved by rose curtains, a silver-grey carpet and light and elegant furniture in the French style. Lady Angel was toying with her embroidery and Prue was trying to mend a fan she had dropped at a rout. The twins were at the window, watching the busy street, one of their favourite occupations.

''Tis strange the dear Duke should have forgotten his promise to call upon us,' Lady Angel remarked.

Prue laid down the broken fan. 'Mama, I have wished to speak of him. I do not doubt his reputation has been exaggerated, but Mrs Beauford is a woman of the world and must know there is some truth in what is said of him.'

'Dorcas Beauford does not have the honour of his acquaintance,' Lady Angel retorted. 'The poor creature is vastly jealous. *Her* girls have never been noticed by a member of the higher nobility. Dorcas was ever a jealous woman, and she is bitterly aware how you all outshine those chicken-faced daughters of hers.'

'Nevertheless,' Prue persisted, 'such a man can have no true interest in us, and a closer acquaintance could be unwise. He is not a man Papa would approve of.'

'You are quite out, miss! Pray, what do you know of men?'

'I think this man means no good to us.'

'I forbid you to speak so! Dorcas is right, you speak too wildly for a chit your age! *I* am a judge of character, and I know the Duke is all a noble gentleman should be, and I'll hear no more of this——'

'Mama!' Selina called from the window. 'A chaise has drawn up before the house, with a coat of arms upon the doors, and an excessively fine gentleman is getting out!'

'Dear heaven! The Duke!' Lady Angel exclaimed, thrusting aside her embroidery to spring to her feet. 'And I in my morning gown and cap! You must receive him, Prue, since you are the eldest! Keep him till I have changed. Lizzie! Lizzie! Where is the wretched creature?' She fled from the room.

Prue felt her heart miss a beat, but there was no time to escape. Her sisters were giggling and pulling their curls in order in a twitter of excitement. She would have to receive him, and endure his insolent glances and repel his unwanted attentions.

The footman opened the door and announced with sonorous relish.

'His Grace the Duke of Carlington.'

He came into the room, a tall, smiling gentleman very gorgeously attired in silver-grey satin. A cravat of finest lawn swathed his throat and ruffles of delicate lace showed at his wrists. He paused to survey the room, then bowed and advanced.

'Good morning, ladies. I trust you have fully recovered from the rigours of your journey?'

Prue rose and curtsied. 'We are honoured, Your Grace. Pray be seated. My mother will be with us in a few minutes, she has been detained upon household matters.'

'Then pray do not hurry her.' He inclined his head and walked to the window. 'Are London streets still a novelty to you young ladies?'

Selina was too overcome to speak, but Cassie said, 'Yes, your Grace. There is always something diverting to be seen.'

'More diverting than is to be seen in Northumberland?'

'Oh yes!' Cassie looked up at him, her blue eyes laughing and her golden curls tumbling about her shoulders. 'I suppose it takes more than a street scene to amuse Your Grace?'

'No, like you I can find amusement in trifling events,' he said easily. 'Now, that old woman trying to stop a dog fight . . .'

They bent to the window, the girls laughing and exclaiming.

Prue stood quite still, an extraordinary medley of emotions surging through her. She had been prepared to chill his advances, to snub him, and here he was positively ignoring her and gazing with undisguised admiration upon Cassie's golden beauty!

She turned hastily as her mother entered the room. 'I–I have a letter to write. . . .'

'Prue, I insist——' her mother began, but Prue had slipped out of the room.

In her bedroom she sank upon a chair, breathing fast. He was as Mrs Beauford had said, a libertine! His grey eyes had been cool when they met hers and he had turned away as soon as he could. Now it was Cassie whom he favoured with his notice! No doubt Selina would be the next!

She waited until she saw the ducal carriage drive off, then she returned to the drawing-room and her mother's angry reproaches.

'Such a display of gauche manners! For very shame I had to pretend you were taken with the vapours! That a daughter of mine should so forget herself!'

'La, he was vastly easy,' Selina declared, her eyes sparkling. 'He is to take us to Vauxhall Gardens, is that not prime? I'm perfectly at home with him, even though he's a Duke.'

'Wait until Minnie and Caro hear of it,' Cassie chuckled, smoothing her gown. 'He complimented me upon this muslin and said he had never seen prettier.'

When she was alone with her sisters Prue could not help asking, 'Did the Duke make any comment upon my—my disappearance?'

'Oh faith, he said you looked somewhat out of countenance and perchance London did not suit you,' Selina said carelessly. 'Cassie, what gowns shall we wear to Vauxhall?'

Prue turned away. She had been right about him, and she should be grateful that she was no longer an object of interest to a man she despised. That, surely, was what she wished? But honesty made her confess the truth.

'I planned to give him a set-down,' she thought ruefully, 'and he turned the tables on me. But he is still dangerous to my sisters and my bemused mother. I *must* make Mama understand how it is; that he could ruin our chances in society if we were seen in his company too often. To be objects of his casual attentions . . . No! It shall not be!'

She began to look for the work she had been engaged upon.

'Are you searching for your fan?' Cassie asked. 'His Grace took it when we told him you had broken it. He says he knows where it can be mended.'

'*Most* condescending of him,' Selina added.

Prue's eyes flashed and colour stained her cheeks. 'I do not want his condescension!'

'La, sister, what are you about?' Cassie stared at her. 'Times I do not know what to think of you.'

Prue turned away quickly. There were times when she did not know what to make of herself either! She had determined to banish all thought of His Grace the Duke of Carlington, and here she was, wishing she had not rushed off in so childish a manner, positively as if she were afraid of him!

How it must have amused him! She pictured the mocking laughter in his eyes as she had whisked out of the room, and she felt her cheeks burn with mortification. And now she was going to be forced to endure a whole evening in his company when he took them to sample the delights of Vauxhall Gardens!

# CHAPTER FOUR

LADY ANGEL would not be persuaded that the evening at Vauxhall Gardens under the Duke's patronage might be unwise, and Prue, when she announced she would not attend the outing, had her ears soundly boxed and was told she would be sent back to Northumberland if she persisted in being so wilful.

There was no help for it, Prue saw, she would have to go. The twins were in a twitter of excitement and the days were filled with anxious consultations of what gowns would be most suitable to mark the occasion of such flattering notice on the Duke's part. Lady Angel, secure in the knowledge that her family diamonds were as good as anyone's and her purple brocade polonaise and cream satin petticoat in high fashion, was more tranquil, but Cassie and Selina changed their minds twenty times a day.

'My blue, perhaps,' Selina mused, 'but I think it makes me a trifle sallow. Do you think so, Cassie?'

But Cassie was twirling before a mirror, intent on observing the fall of pink striped satin at the back of her gown, and called to Lizzie to come and pin it tighter at the neck.

'Prue, you are to wear your cream taffeta,' Lady Angel ordered, 'and use some virgin milk for your complexion, it is still too highly coloured.'

'Thank you, ma'am,' Prue's mouth took on a mutinous air, 'but I have no wish for a fashionable pallor—and I do not care what gown I wear, as I have no expectation of pleasure in the party.'

She was in the morning-room, playing on Aunt Fanny's spinet, when a footman came in with a packet which, he said, had come by special messenger. Prue opened it and caught her breath as she drew from the wrappings a most exquisite fan painted with rosy cherubs and garlanded goddesses. The sticks were of carved ivory and as delicate as lace. There was a note with it. *'It is with regret, Mistress Prue, that I report your broken fan is beyond repairing. As a sword is to a man, so is a fan to a beauty, and I beg you will accept this trifle as a sincere token of the honour I feel you and your family bestow upon me by allowing me to display some of the pleasant amusements of Vauxhall Gardens this evening. Carlington.'*

Before she could gather her thoughts, her mother entered the room and caught up the fan with an exclamation of delight.

'Such a beauty! So elegant a design, such noble taste! From the Duke, of course. I saw his chaise drive off.'

'I cannot accept it!' Prue jumped up. 'He has no right to send me such a gift! I do not want it—and I shall return it to him!'

Lady Angel laid the fan down and for a moment she did not speak. Then she said, tight-lipped, 'You have taken a most ill-judged dislike to His Grace the Duke and I shall not allow it, miss! When you wish to insult him by returning his charming gift, and refuse his invitation, you think entirely of yourself in a highly selfish manner. Yes, selfish and *wicked*! Do you never think how your sisters shall benefit by the Duke's interest in us? That it will open important doors for us all and set a seal upon our position in society?'

'I do not think the Duke's interest will do us aught but harm, seeing he is an acknowledged rake.'

'Fustian! The Duke, miss, is as other men are. You are uncommonly innocent if you do not know the temptations that men such as he face, and how easy it is for them to yield! We do not expect men of high degree to be models of morality. Men are sadly lustful, they have their mistresses and light o' loves, but it has nothing to do with us.

'Such men will respect purity in a woman. The Duke's attentions are highly honourable and we are deeply grateful for them! You will thank him for his gift with proper respect, and show no more of this mutinous and naughty spirit!'

That evening, dressed in a cream satin gown with ruchings of sapphire velvet around the square-cut *décolletage*, the skirt looped to show a blue-and-gold striped petticoat, Prue surveyed her reflection in her looking-glass. Lizzie had arranged her dark curls high, with a posy of tiny cream rosebuds tucked in at the side.

'Faith, I'm growing vain,' she told herself as she caught up a scarf of Chambray gauze. 'Unless I beware, I shall get the notion I'm a beauty.' She chuckled and took the Duke's fan and a satin reticule from Lizzie, and went down to join her mother and sisters. The twins looked delightful in their innocent pink and blue gowns, their eyes sparkling as they peered out of the window.

'The coach is here!' they cried, and with a prodigious rustling of silks and exhortations from Lizzie on the dangers of the night air, they descended to the hall. A footman in the Duke's livery of black and silver escorted them to the coach, where the Duke awaited them.

Prue sat in a corner, drawing her cloak around her. In spite of her qualms, she could not prevent her spirits rising as the stately coach rumbled over the cobbles. Vauxhall Gardens! What dreams she had nursed of walking its lamplit paths, and listening to music and eating supper in some fairylike grove!

The twins were in an ecstasy of joy, whispering and darting their eyes on every side, afraid of missing some excitement. Stars had appeared in the purple sky and a moon rose above the trees, its pale light picking out the Greek statuary and miniature temples when they entered the gardens.

They crossed the Grove and strolled to the concert hall

where an orchestra was playing. They were early, and as yet the modish crowd had not gathered. The Duke found seats for them and proceeded to converse with Lady Angel. So far he had not glanced in Prue's direction and she could not help, most illogically, feeling somewhat nettled by his lack of interest! Of course it was what she wanted, that he should lose any interest he had in her, but good manners surely demanded something more than apparent unawareness of her presence!

Suddenly he turned and spoke directly to her.

'May I be allowed the honour of showing you the illuminated fountain, Mistress Prue? 'Tis a graceful conceit.'

'Go, Prue my dear,' Lady Angel said, smiling upon her. 'I'm sure it is vastly kind of His Grace.'

Prue hesitated, then rose, curtsied, and laid her fingers lightly upon the silver-grey satin sleeve extended to her, and they proceeded to walk along a path lit by painted Chinese lanterns strung through the trees. Couples were strolling past them, the light catching jewels, buckles and sword-hilts. The soft air caressed Prue's bare neck and arms, and as she looked around her some of her tension disappeared and turning to the man beside her she said,

'I have to thank Your Grace for your gift. It is indeed a fan such as I have never owned. But you had no necessity to send it.'

'Ah, but I had, Mistress Prue. A beauty must be surrounded with beauty.' He drew closer, looking down at her, a smile on his well-cut lips.

'You are mistaken, Your Grace,' she retorted. 'I am no beauty, my sisters have ever outshone me.'

'Those pretty little pink and gold cherubs?' He put his hand over hers. 'Mistress Prue, do you not know you have a beauty that is rare indeed . . . a magic that compels a man to—respond?'

She looked up into his face and saw that his eyes, no longer smiling, were bent intently on hers. It was a handsome face, strongly boned and powerful, the mouth firm, perhaps even harsh, and a chin that spoke of will-power and obstinacy. The lines of dissipation around eyes and mouth did not detract from the compelling attraction of the man. Prue found she could not tear her eyes away! Something burning deep in his eyes was drawing a response from her and she knew she was in danger.

She stammered: 'Your Grace . . . we should return. . . .'

Suddenly she realised they had turned into one of the many little unlit byways where moonlight filtered only fitfully through the trees. Before she could protest, she found herself caught into his arms and his mouth crushing hers. His lips bruised hers in hot passion, and she felt his hand caress her breast.

'No!' She strained away from him, fighting him with all her strength. 'Let me go, sir! You shall not . . .' She twisted in his arms, seeking escape. Blood pounded through her body as unknown, terrifying emotions rose in her. She was imprisoned, by his passion and her own weakness. She cried out and fell forward upon his breast. 'Let me go. . . . In God's name, let me go!'

For a second, as she lay against him feeling the hard male strength of his body against hers, her weakness threatened to overcome her and she knew she was near to surrendering to him. Then, abruptly, his arms relaxed and he was holding her gently as she swayed, half fainting.

'Prue, you are dangerous magic to a man,' he said thickly. 'The devil! Someone comes, and 'tis as well you are not seen here . . . with me.'

She shrank away, drawing her scarf around her. 'Take me back, sir. I—I do not care for Your Grace's . . . attentions.'

She swung around and began to walk swiftly back towards the main path.

He caught her up in a few strides. 'Prue, you cannot blame

me. You do not condemn me for failing to resist your loveliness and charm? 'Fore Gód, no man could resist you, I swear!'

She had regained control over her agitation, although her heart was still thudding in her breast and her breath came jerkily as she said, 'I do blame you! You have insulted me beyond forgiving! I thought you a man of honour, now I realise you know nothing of honour, only hateful lust!'

'What man is without lust, my dear?' She stiffened at the mockery in his voice. 'You have not been kissed before, I think, my little dark-eyed witch.' He drew close, taking her hand. 'You have much to learn and I . . . am an excellent teacher.'

She snatched her hand away. 'Never! I do not wish ever to see you again! I . . . I despise you and—and hate you!'

'Faith, a woman who hates deeply can be won to love deeply. Sweet child, you stirred my heart from the moment I saw you.'

'Enough, sir. I thought you a gentleman.' She turned to face him. 'I find you a boor! I have neither father nor brother with me to protect me, and you take advantage of it!'

'Wait, Prue——' he began, but she walked past him, her head high and her cheeks burning.

The rest of the evening was painful for her. To pretend she was enjoying the music and strolling among the gay crowds, to talk and smile and try to eat the elegant repast served them, took all her strength. The Duke remained his urbane self, charming Lady Angel and the twins with compliments, pointing out the well-known personalities of society, stage and the sporting world, and recounting wicked little scandals relating to them.

At last the hateful evening was over for Prue. She escaped into the house while her mother was expressing her grateful thanks and the twins were making it plain they hoped it was not going to be the last invitation to be offered.

She tore off her dress and flung it on the floor. In her nightgown, her dark curls tumbled about her shoulders, she stared at herself in the glass once again and saw a different girl. The Prue she knew had gone for ever. The dark-eyed girl in the mirror had an alive, vivid, warm beauty that had been born of a man's harsh kiss. Tonight had made her a woman, a woman who had felt the hot stir of passion in a man's arms. Now she must beware of her womanhood; she must learn to guard her passions, control her instincts lest they betray her.

The Duke had said she had beauty, and a dangerous magic. Were they to bring her danger, perhaps shame? Her father had warned her, and she would heed his warning and trust no man till he proved himself worthy of her trust.

Suddenly she was deadly weary, and was deep in sleep when Lizzie came to ask if she wished some hot milk to compose her nerves after the excitement of the evening.

It was some days after the expedition to Vauxhall Gardens, and the twins were still discussing the delights. Prue had tried, without success, to thrust memories of the evening aside, but her blood stirred when she recalled the Duke's demanding kisses and the strength of his arms imprisoning her. She knew it might spell disaster if she told her mother what had happened that night. Either Lady Angel, unwilling to believe the Duke an unsuitable acquaintance and see the end to her rosy dreams, would accuse her of flirting or misunderstanding his attentions; or she would put herself into a fine pucker and have the vapours and drag her husband to London to avenge the family's honour! Either course of action could lead to trouble, and the latter probably to banishment to Northumberland, and Prue knew that she did not wish to leave London.

She was in her mother's bedroom one morning, watching her riffling through her letters.

'We have an invitation to cards with the Honourable Mrs Audley for Friday night; I expect there will be dancing for the younger folk. I see Dorcas asks us to dine next week. . . .' Lady Angel picked up a letter. 'Here's a hand I do not know.' She broke the wafer, glanced at the letter and exclaimed,

'Well 'pon honour, here's a surprise, daughter! 'Tis a letter from a nephew of Fanny's husband! Harry Dunstan, I remember she once spoke of him. A worthy young man, I believe, but of no consequence.' She tossed the letter aside. 'He desires to call upon us. No doubt he was disappointed when he did not get the whole of poor Fanny's estate, and has it in his mind to try and get something from us. I'll have nothing to do with him.'

Prue took the letter and read it with interest. 'He writes well and expresses suitable sentiments, Mama. I think you judge him too harshly. He is a connection of ours, and it would be unkind to refuse him.'

Cassie, who had come into the room, peered over Prue's shoulder.

'La, there's a portrait of him in the library. Let us be friendly, Mama, or he will think us too set-up to know him.'

'I do not care what he thinks of us,' her mother replied tartly. 'However, I shall consider it. We can always send him packing if he's a ramshackle fellow.'

Cassie tugged at Prue's sleeve. 'Come, Sis, and look at Harry Dunstan's portrait.'

They went down to the library and Prue stared up at a portrait to which she had not paid much attention. She saw a young man in a green coat with lightly powdered hair. Something in his face attracted her; the chin was firm and the dark eyes and brows had a certain distinction.

''Tis a face I would trust,' she said thoughtfully.

'Do you think Mama *will* invite him to call?' Cassie asked anxiously.

Prue laughed. 'If we plague her enough. I think I like Mr

Harry Dunstan, even if he is of little consequence.'

Cassie was gazing up at the portrait and as Prue turned away she heard her sister murmur: 'I've often wondered who he was. Harry . . . I like the name; I like *him*! Oh, we *must* ask him to visit us, I long to meet him! There is something about him. . . .'

Startled, Prue looked back. Her sister was looking at the portrait and something in her face made Prue uneasy. Cassie fell in love easily, and it would be disastrous if she were to lose her heart to a man, no matter how respectable, who had neither fortune nor high place in society. Had it been a mistake to suggest that Lady Angel should allow Harry Dunstan to call?

'Cassie——' she began, but Cassie had advanced, kissed the tip of a finger and laid it lightly on the mouth of the man in the painting.

'Oh, Prue, I feel he's mine now!' She laughed and spun around. 'I've kissed him and he can't escape! And if you tell Mama, I'll never forgive you, *never*!' She danced out of the room, leaving Prue to follow her thoughtfully.

# CHAPTER FIVE

THE DUKE sent to enquire how the ladies were after the entertainment at the Gardens, and some days later he called upon them, bringing his private secretary, a slim, fair young man with a reserved manner who remained unobtrusively in the background, but whose eyes, Prue noticed, were quietly taking note of them all. His name was John Hillier.

'John keeps me from making my worst blunders,' His Grace remarked lazily, seating himself on the settee beside Lady Angel, 'he has the ability to disentangle me from the unfortunate passes into which I sometimes fall, a quality making him highly valuable to me.'

He produced a gold snuff-box set with diamonds, and tapped it delicately before taking a pinch of snuff. 'He is my memory, and my conscience.' He threw the young man a mocking glance. 'The last, I fear, causes him some inconvenience, not to say moral suffering.'

Mr Hillier bowed slightly, then turned to ask Selina how she had enjoyed Vauxhall.

Prue, sitting on a stool near her mother, had no illusions about why the Duke was there. His eyes were on her whenever she looked up, and she knew he had seen her colour rise and was amused. She attempted to join Selina, but her mother called her back to answer the Duke's questions about Aunt Fanny's library.

'Alack, I am sadly ignorant, Your Grace,' Lady Angel sighed. 'I get little time for literature with my domestic and social duties, but Prue is a true bookworm.'

'Indeed, ma'am,' Prue said hastily, 'I have not tried to read any of the volumes.'

'Nay, I'm sure you have inspected the collection,' the Duke said, rising. 'Pray allow me to see your library, Mistress Prue.'

She bit her lip. 'Very well, Your Grace, but I assure you it is of very little interest.'

He followed her out of the room and down to the library. With her hand on the door she turned, meeting his eyes directly.

'Your Grace, I am not taken in by your professed interest in my aunt's library.'

His brows rose, quizzing her. 'Am I so transparent? Then pray tell me why I should practise deceit, ma'am.'

'You wish to be alone with me,' she told him bluntly, 'and I, sir, have no wish to be alone with you.' Her glance went meaningly to the porter in his hall chair. 'I have help within call this time . . . should I need it.'

He nodded approvingly. 'A woman of spirit; I like that. Come, let us talk more privately; your door is not so thick but a cry of virtue assailed will reach your servant.'

Prue flung open the door and they entered. She went to stand by the window while the Duke glanced at the book-lined walls, and then strolled over to join her.

'As you remarked, not a collection of distinction, I think. Mistress Prue, am I not to be forgiven? You have no manner of right to be so tempting and then rebuke me for failing to resist you. Come,' he held out his hand, his grey eyes amused, 'do not play the prude, sweet lady. You resisted my kisses—but were they so truly hateful to you?'

When she backed away, her hands behind her back, he said with a change of tone: 'I think you have not considered how much may be gained by my patronage. Your esteemed mother wishes to enter society, and your sisters, no doubt, hope for suitable husbands. It is in my power——'

'It is in your power to ruin us all!' Prue flung up her head. 'Your reputation will assure it. We shall be suspected of being objects of your libertine pursuit!'

'What, *all* of you?' he asked in mock horror. 'I grant you your lady mother is in fine preservation, and your sisters most sweet little doves. . . .'

'You choose to be insulting!' She turned away, fearing her anger might make her cast all caution aside. 'I most earnestly desire Your Grace to leave us alone to find society of our own choosing.'

'But I have no wish to leave *you*,' he said softly. 'You are an angel spiced with the devil, and I cannot resist you.'

'You would ruin me, sir?'

He came close and she felt herself tremble. 'I would love you—and make you love me, Prue. You have not known love; I shall teach you.'

'I—I have no wish to be so taught!' Anger gave her courage to face him. 'I suspect you have taught many unfortunate women, and to their undoing! Do not waste your time on me! 'Twill be better appreciated by the Muslin Company!'

She walked swiftly from the room. The footman was in the hall and she called to him: 'Escort His Grace to the drawing-room.' She turned and dropped the Duke a curtsey. 'I fear I must leave you, I have duties to perform.'

She hurried away, leaving him standing looking after her with a curious expression on his handsome face.

To her relief the Duke appeared to accept defeat, and Lady Angel grew pettish waiting for another visit from him. Prue knew that her mother had not given up hopes of using his influence to further her plans, and still, possibly, entertained the delightful prospect of having a ducal son-in-law.

Mr Harry Dunstan was graciously invited to call at Grosvenor Street, and duly presented himself one morning when the ladies were seated at their work in the morning-room. Lady Angel greeted him coolly, still suspicious of intentions to try and deprive her of her inheritance, but Prue liked this square-faced, well-set-up young man in plain brown coat and buff breeches, and she made him welcome while Cassie subsided into a flutter of excitement that held her silent for some moments.

'I believe you were much attached to our aunt,' Prue said, smiling at him. She was wearing a pale blue lutestring gown with a dainty lace apron, and felt pleased that she had put on her most becoming cap of pleated lawn and rose ribbons. 'I hope it does not distress you to see us settled in her house.'

He bowed. 'No, ma'am, not in the least. I was saddened by my aunt's death, but she had been failing in health for some years, so it was not unexpected. I am truly glad that through her generosity you have been able to enjoy the pleasures of London.'

Lady Angel chose to take exception to this.

'Indeed, sir, 'twas only right that my sister should *at last* have taken notice of her own flesh and blood!'

He bowed again, and turning to Prue, asked what entertainments they had attended and Cassie, overcoming her shyness, joined eagerly in the conversation. Presently Prue went to give orders to the footman to bring sherry and biscuits for their guest. When she returned, Cassie was gazing with breathless adoration at the young man as he made the tentative suggestion he should escort them to a display of fireworks to be held on the river Thames that evening.

'Oh, Mama, *may* we go?' Cassie implored, sliding an arm around her mother's neck. 'I would like it beyond everything!'

'Indeed yes, dear Mama,' Selina begged. 'We have never seen such a display, and all London will be there.'

Prue added her pleas and Lady Angel, prompted more by her own wish to be seen among 'all London' than her daughters' longings, gave her consent. They would be pleased to accept Mr Dunstan's invitation to ride with him to the display.

''Twill be but a hired coach, I fear,' he said bluntly. 'My circumstances do not permit my keeping an equipage.'

Lady Angel stiffened slightly. 'Then we shall go in *our* coach, it is sufficient for all of us, and Lawson is most knowledgeable about London streets.'

The evening proved delightful. Prue was enchanted with the brilliant patterns of the rockets reflected in the dark waters of the river.

Lady Angel caught sight of her friend, Mrs Beauford and her daughters in their coach and whispered to Prue, ''Tis most unfortunate we are not with the dear Duke. Dorcas pretends to believe that I invent his acquaintance.'

Prue's eyes had been busy. She persuaded herself she was not looking for anyone especially, but once when a tall, broad-shouldered man in silver-grey drove past in a small landaulette, she felt her heart jump in her breast and knew she hoped to see the man she had decided to hate.

Cassie came into Prue's room that night. Her blue eyes were dreamy as she perched herself on the bed, sighing rapturously, 'He is much, *much* more handsome than his portrait! Did you not think so, Prue?'

Prue paused in brushing her curls. 'I'm afraid I don't consider him very handsome. But I like him, I think he has a good character and most pleasant manners.'

'Oh, I think Harry is of the first water! So entertaining and easy to talk to, so thoughtful. . . .' She frowned suddenly. 'He was somewhat attentive to you—but of course you are the eldest, and it was his duty to be respectful to you and Mama.'

Prue laughed. 'Oh, naturally he had to restrain his first inclination and concentrate upon the matrons of the party.'

'Well, I did not mean that exactly. He did look at you a lot. . . .'

'He was obliged to,' Prue said, jumping into bed, 'I told him I would see he was not invited here again unless he did!'

'Prue, you're hoaxing me!' Cassie prepared to leave. 'I shall tell him he has done his duty and can now ignore you and pay attention to me. Goodnight, sister.'

Harry Dunstan did not wait to be invited again. He called often at Grosvenor Street and escorted his cousins—as he called them—on shopping expeditions and to concerts. He worked as a barrister in the law courts, and Prue discovered that he had ambitions and guessed, also, the ability to achieve them. She enjoyed his company and his friendly acceptance of their demands to be taken to see the sights of the city, and to partner them to assemblies.

She thought he showed a partiality for her, something that sent Cassie into the sulks at times. Her sister had made her infatuation a trifle too obvious, causing the young man to retreat into a safer companionship with Prue.

After some heavy hinting, Mrs Beauford had reluctantly obtained invitations for the Angel family to a ball to be given by Sir Edwin and Lady Delain in St James's Square, a most fashionable quarter of the town, and the Misses Beauford came to take tea with their friends and discuss hair-styles and gowns for the event.

'Small hoops, of course,' Miss Caro pronounced, 'the large are for court wear only.'

'You know, of course, that hair must now be raised in front more and twisted into a back knot,' Miss Minnie said. 'Feathers, jewels *and* bows to trim it, naturally.'

'I prefer a simpler style,' Prue said carelessly. She found that the Misses Beauford irritated her and their conversation bored her.

Minnie tittered. ''Tis as well, since Monsieur Jules takes only special clients.'

Caro was eyeing Prue slyly. 'Do you intend to dance with the Duke of Carlington? He will be there, because my Lady Anastasia Storrington attends and 'tis perfectly well known she is his present mistress.'

'One of many, 'tis said,' Minnie added. 'Mrs Bruton, the Honourable Mrs Allen, the little Spanish dancer.... Of course you must know the Duke is called the Perfidious Devil? Such a scandalous creature! I quite tremble for you if you become the object of his attention!'

'Well that's a chuffy thing to say!' Cassie declared roundly. 'The Duke has ever behaved with propriety towards us.'

So the Duke would be at the ball! Prue felt a tiny shiver of excitement. Of course she hated him, and despised him for a heartless libertine and a danger to all virtuous women, yet the prospect of meeting him again, of catching his eyes upon her with that curious burning look she had surprised in them before, made her blood race and her pulse flutter unevenly.

Perhaps, she thought, trying to calm her agitation, if she were to see him with his mistress, it would cure her of this unhappy disturbance of mind when she thought of meeting him. He meant her no good, of that she was certain! He wished to teach her to love! It was possible he desired her—but not as a wife, that *never*!

Two weeks later, as she waited with her mother and sisters in the long line of coaches in St James's Square, Prue's head was hot and her hands cold, and under the cherry satin of her charming gown her heart beat quickly. She turned her head lest the others notice her agitation, but they were too busy observing the notabilities in other carriages.

'Look, Selina, there is the Signorina we heard at the Opera last week! Mama, just see her pearls!'

'And there is that handsome lord who took the famous Fanny Murray as his——'

'Hush, Selina! Such scandalous talk! You should know nothing of such things,' Lady Angel exclaimed in shocked reproof.

'La, Fanny is respectably married to the actor, David Ross, now,' Cassie giggled, 'but she was *very* scandalous in her day!'

Once inside the Delain residence, the slow procession in the reception line and dazzling brilliance of light from a dozen crystal chandeliers made Prue feel she had entered another world, a world of fairylike luxury lit by hundreds of candles and heavy with the scents of French perfume, powder and hot-house flowers.

She caught her breath in delight as she followed her mother into the long ballroom where great banks of blooms filled every window embrasure, and walls hung with pale blue satin damask held Venetian mirrors that caught and returned the magnificence of the scene before them. Satins and brocades, laces and feathers, diamond buckles blazed around her. Never had she beheld such splendour! Cassie and Selina stared, dumbfounded, and even Lady Angel's composure was shaken for a moment.

'Come, daughters. I see dear Dorcas and her girls, we shall sit with them and discover who some of the guests are.' She surged forward, formidable in green brocade and towering head-dress of feathers and satin ribbons.

But Mrs Beauford was protecting her girls from any unhappy comparison with their attractive friends. From amid a group, she called out, 'Oh, sweetest Clarissa, you come too late to join us, I fear! See, every chair is taken. But you will doubtless find something in the card-room.'

'May I escort you ladies to the far end?' Harry Dunstan asked from behind them. 'I see empty seats there.'

'Oh, Mr Dunstan, you are vastly kind,' Lady Angel said gratefully, and after bestowing a less than fond look upon her dearest Dorcas, she and her daughters followed Harry and found comfortable seats from where they could observe the brilliant company.

'No doubt you are surprised to see me here,' Harry said, smiling at Prue. 'I am friendly with our hostess's younger son, who generously procured me an invitation.'

'Indeed, I am excessively glad he did,' Prue said frankly, 'for we know no one here, and 'tis the first grand ball I have attended.'

'May I have the honour of a dance later?' he asked.

'Are you not going to ask *me* to dance?' Cassie asked sharply. 'Prue is the eldest, so of course you must stand up with her first, but once you have done so you are——'

'You are free, Mr Dunstan,' Prue chuckled. 'Free to cast dull duty to the winds and enjoy yourself!'

'Oh, Mistress Prue, you must know—' but Prue, catching Cassie's angry stare, had turned to talk to an acquaintance she had recently met at the Beaufords' and whom she now invited to sit with her.

Suddenly she heard her friend exclaim: 'Ah, he's come at last, the Perfidious Devil himself! And she is with him! Quite shameless, of course. My dear Mistress Prue, pray observe our most distinguished rake!'

Prue felt her heart jerk as she turned her head. His Grace the Duke of Carlington was standing in the entrance, glancing around him with faintly arrogant interest, and on his arm was the most beautiful woman Prue had ever seen.

''Tis said his carriage is often at her door,' her friend hissed in her ear. 'Oh for sure, he deserves his name. Beware of him, sweet child, if you value your good name.'

'I—I know His Grace but slightly,' Prue murmured, and turned away swiftly, but not before the Duke had looked across the room and their eyes had met.

# CHAPTER SIX

PRUE went to stand up with Harry in a country dance. While they waited for the music to change, he said abruptly, 'Mistress Prue, at the risk of your thinking me impertinent and over-nice in my tastes, I must warn you against the attentions that the Duke of Carlington has seen fit to bestow on your family. I know he calls upon you, and has taken you to Vauxhall. I cannot believe your mother to be aware of his reputation.'

'My mother knows well what is said of him,' Prue sighed, 'but I fear she is somewhat dazzled by such attentions. It is unlikely, however, that he will continue to acknowledge us; he has other interests.' Her eyes went to the beautiful Lady Anastasia hanging on to the Duke's arm and laughing up into his face.

Harry said no more, but she thought he continued to look uneasy and she felt gratitude for his concern, a concern which would have been much greater if he had known *all* the Duke's attentions!

Selina was in a group of people, looking flushed and happy, with a tall, handsome man standing beside her smiling down at her. Lady Angel whispered behind her fan,

'Selina lost a ribbon from her hair and this gentleman rescued it, and begged to make himself known to us. Sir Joseph Meryton, a most genteel and polished gentleman. He introduced us to his wife and sister-in-law, are we not lucky?'

'He looks a sensible man,' Prue said, 'and his wife is pretty, if a trifle wispish.'

'The dear Duke is here,' her mother said. 'Have you seen him? He is with that horrid Lady Anastasia! It is strange he has not presented himself to us.'

'Mama, I have told you that the Duke may not acknowledge us in high society, 'tis not to be expected ... and perhaps it is as well for us.'

'Pray do not be tiresome, Prue! I forbid you to speak in such a way. It will *not* be well should he drop us, I could not face Dorcas if such a thing happened! She is vastly envious, and keeps prating of his supposed rakish behaviour. As if any man as high as he in the world has not such rakishness attached to him by jealous females. I will not consent to any of it; rumour is ever unreliable.'

A young man came up, bowed to Prue and asked her to dance, and, glad to get away from her mother's scolding, she went with him to the centre of the room. As she chatted idly, she suddenly felt that she was being watched and turning her head, saw the Duke standing alone by a door that led into the lantern-lit garden.

She looked away quickly, but her calm was shaken and she had to force herself to keep her attention on the dance and her partner. As the dance ended and they moved away, the Duke's secretary, John Hillier, approached, bowed and murmured something to Prue's partner who turned and said,

'I must pray you to excuse me, ma'am, my presence is requested.... This gentleman will escort you to your place.'

He hurried off, and as Prue turned to John Hillier she found him vanished and in his place stood the Duke.

He extended his arm and automatically she laid her hand upon it and moved with him to the door.

''Tis unpleasantly hot in here, I think,' he murmured. 'The gardens are quite fine. Have you observed them, Mistress Prue?'

She shook her head, words having deserted her. She could

not protest and make a scene! She would die of shame with so many eyes upon her!

The night air cooled her hot face and the darkness hid her agitation. The music had begun and couples were returning to the ballroom. Tiny fairy lights among the trees and shrubs flickered like so many glow-worms.

They walked in silence for some time. At last the Duke said softly, 'You look very beautiful tonight, Prue, very enchanting . . . and not at all like an angel!'

'You are looking, then, for a sister-devil?' she retorted.

'I have no wish for any sister.' She heard the laughter in his voice. 'So you have heard my undeserved title?'

'Yes, Your Grace—and that it is *not* undeserved.'

'And therefore it intrigues you! No woman can resist a devil, you know, they entertain hopes of reforming him.'

'Alack that I am so unwomanly, for I have no desire whatever to reform you or your ways, my Lord Duke.'

'Your enchantment grows!' He stopped and turned to look down at her. In the dark she could not see his expression. 'You would take me as I am?'

She looked at him levelly. 'I do not intend to take you at all, Your Grace.'

'Perhaps I could make you change your mind . . . by taking *you*, my wilful, lovely little angel!' He caught her hand. His touch sent a shiver through her and she looked away from him lest he see how shaken she was. 'Prue, cease playing with me! 'Fore God, I'll not stand it longer! You drive me mad! You come between me and my pleasures. . . .'

'Even between you and . . . Lady Anastasia?'

'She means nothing; you mean everything!'

She dragged her hand away, her eyes blazing. 'And how soon shall I mean nothing? A week? A month? Perhaps even a year? I find you deeply insulting, sir, and I refuse to listen to you longer!'

As she turned, he caught her by her shoulders, his fingers biting into her soft flesh.

'You *shall* listen to me, Prue! I am offering you no trifling intrigue; I can give you much, a fine establishment, jewels, introduction into a society that——'

'A society that will call me your latest light o' love!' she flung at him. 'You offer me shame and ruin! I have never given you cause to——'

'You have never given me anything, sweet angel, that is what I complain about. Come, you have protested enough! I am not a man to be thwarted! You shall be mine, willing or unwilling!'

He pulled her into his arms. As he bent to kiss her, she cried out and felt his arms slacken as he stepped back, and heard him say furiously, 'What devil's hell brings you here, you young hound?'

Prue saw the shadowy figure of a man behind them.

'I beg pardon, sir,' John Hillier said woodenly. 'The Lady Anastasia.... I observed her entering the garden and ... Lady Anastasia seemed somewhat—discomposed.'

The Duke swore wrathfully. 'In God's name, could you not head her off? You young fool, I——' he turned his head sharply as a light step and a rustle of satin came to his ears.

Prue slipped past him and found her arm caught and held gently as John Hillier murmured,

'To the left, Mistress Angel, there is a path.'

She let him guide her, grateful for the shadows as she sought to compose herself. She wondered if the young secretary could feel how she trembled, and if he guessed the cause. As they came in sight of the house she paused and said quietly,

'You were sent by the Duke, I think, to dismiss my dance partner.'

'I was so ordered.' His voice was low and troubled.

'Yet you came to—to rescue me, did you not?'

'I . . . did perhaps suggest to Lady Anastasia that His Grace was taking the air in the garden.'

Prue pressed his arm. 'Thank you, sir. I am grateful. I hope you will not speak of this to anyone.'

'To no one, I swear.'

'Will the Duke be vastly angry with you?'

A wry smile touched his lips. 'It is possible that he may decide to dispense with my services after tonight.'

'Oh, I would not have that!' she cried, dismayed.

'Your concern for me, Mistress Angel, is something I shall ever treasure.' He raised her hand to his lips, then led her into the ballroom and to where her mother sat conversing with several richly dressed matrons.

'La, child where have you been?' her mother demanded. ''Tis time we supped, and Mr Dunstan and Sir Joseph wait to escort us.'

Prue looked around her. 'Does Lady Meryton not come with us?'

'I fear my wife suffers from a delicate constitution,' Sir Joseph told her, bowing, 'she cannot take rich food, and is now playing cards.'

'Oh, do let us hurry!' Selina exclaimed, eagerly clutching the arm Sir Joseph extended, 'I vow I'm famished!'

He looked slightly taken aback and murmured: 'Your mother . . .'

'Oh, Mr Harry will arm her in,' Selina declared, urging him towards the door. 'Let us find a good place before all are filled.'

As they moved off, Cassie pinched Prue's arm and whispered, 'I am positively ashamed of her! She has been making such a play for him, and Mama does not seem to heed. He is a married man.'

'But not particularly attentive to his wife,' Prue said, frowning. 'Selina often puts me to the blush, she has little sense in her head.'

'I'm not so much better,' Cassie said frankly, 'but I do not seek to attach married men.'

'No,' Prue murmured, 'only pleasant young gentlemen engaged in law.'

'You are quizzing me, sister,' Cassie rebuked her, her eyes going to Harry Dunstan, who was steering her mother in the direction of the dining-room.

The tables were set with crystal, silver and baskets of delicate sweetmeats and a magnificent variety of food, but Prue could eat little, and when Harry remarked on her lack of appetite she was forced to pretend the heat of the ballroom had made her head ache.

She must get through the evening somehow without revealing the turmoil of anger and mortification the Duke's offer had aroused in her. When she returned to the ballroom she refused partners, pleading fatigue, and indeed by now her head was truly aching and weariness claimed her. At last her mother rose and, to Prue's vast relief, declared it time to leave. Only Selina, in close confabulation with Sir Joseph Meryton, protested, and was not calmed until he had promised to call upon them the next day.

'With your wife, of course,' Lady Angel said, smiling on him graciously.

Sir Joseph bowed his thanks, and they left the ballroom and called for their coach.

Sunk in a corner of the coach, her cloak wrapped around her, Prue let her pent-up feelings rush over her. How dared the Duke offer her such a shameful life? What had she ever done to make him suppose she would agree to be his mistress? Her whole body seemed afire as she thought of his insolent words, his assurance he meant to have her, willing or unwilling! Because he was one of England's great Dukes and she an insignificant little nobody, he would take her as lightly as he would take one of the poor wretches who wandered the streets at night!

She burned with shame and anger. She would never speak to him again! She would warn her mother....

She glanced at Lady Angel nodding in her corner, a smile of gratification still lingering on her face. Would she believe the Duke's evil intentions? And if she did, and appealed to her husband, what might be the end of it? For Sir Roland—delicate, elderly and no swordsman—a duel was out of the question. They would all be whisked back to Northumberland with Jim West, Selina's rustic admirer, for male company! No, she must hide the shame of the Duke's offer, and avoid him as if he were indeed the devil.

As she lay sleepless that night, she had a sudden memory of cool young lips touching her hand and a low voice saying, 'Your concern for me, Mistress Angel, is something I shall ever treasure', and she thought gratefully of the young secretary's understanding of his master's intention in getting her away from the ballroom, and in alerting Lady Anastasia.

'He did it for me,' she thought, 'and may lose his position with the Duke because of it, alas! I wonder, did he tell Lady Anastasia His Grace was not alone?'

She recalled the beauty's triumphant glances around the room as she stood with her hand on the Duke's arm, and the possessive air with which she tapped him with her fan and laughed up into his handsome face. Lady Anastasia was headstrong, and probably jealous. Would she have made a scene if she had come upon the Duke with a pretty country miss in his arms?

Prue pushed the hair off her hot forehead. She had resisted those arms, but she had felt their strength and some secret part of her had fiercely rejoiced. She hated him, the Perfidious Devil who would ruin her, who swore to have her, and yet still she felt his arms around her, and saw the light in his eyes as he sought her lips!

'There lies my greatest danger,' she thought, staring into the darkness and feeling the heavy beat of her heart shake her. 'I despise him! I hate him! But I fear him most of all, and—dear heaven—I fear myself!'

# CHAPTER SEVEN

'LA, Prue, you look uncommon pale and pinched this morning,' Cassie observed as the sisters sat at a late breakfast. 'Mama's in a pettish way, too, after last night's excitement and a trifle too much champagne, and will not rise till noon, she declares.'

'I found the ballroom overhot and it made my head ache,' Prue told her, sipping her coffee, 'and I did not sleep well.'

'But you enjoyed the ball, surely?' Selina asked, taking another scone. 'Laws, 'twas the best evening's entertainment I've spent! Such elegant company! Such flowers! Such a supper! So many handsome bucks ogling one!' She giggled. 'I was quite put to the blush by some of them. But then, I was in good looks last night, Sir Joseph said I outshone all those simpering debutantes.'

'Sir Joseph Meryton seems an elegant figure of a man,' Prue said thoughtfully. ''Tis a pity his wife is so delicate.'

'Oh, she's a poor creature,' Selina said carelessly, 'she does not care to dance.'

'So you were able to partner him,' Cassie remarked, 'twice—or was it three times? Be careful, sister, he's a married man and you'll get yourself talked about.'

Selina tossed her head. 'La, how you do run on! Mama was all approval. Sir Joseph is a man of most respectable reputation and sensibility, and he has *such* a fund of amusing anecdotes about society. He had me in a choke of laughter, I declare!'

Prue relapsed into silence, letting her sisters chatter on

about the ball and their partners. The feelings that had banished sleep still persisted. That the Duke should have thought her so easy a victim! That he saw no insult in his behaviour towards her! That he expected any woman to accept his infamous offers with gratitude, nay—delight! Well, she would make it plain that here was one woman who rejected his so-called love!

Unbidden, his words came back to her: 'You shall be mine, willing or unwilling. . . .'

She pushed her cup aside and rose, saying: 'I shall see how Mama is this morning.'

She found Lady Angel risen and in a fine tweak.

'Oh, heavens, it had escaped me! Naturally the gentlemen will be calling to ask how we do after the ball! 'Twill not be in order for you girls to receive company alone. Go, Prue, and change your morning gown for something better . . . and send Lizzie to me. Is my chintz gown pressed? Where is my lemon-water? Hurry, child, and tell your sisters they are to receive no one till I am with them.'

'I beg you will excuse me, Mama, I feel a trifle unwell——'

'Tush, you have a fine colour! Put yourself in order and join us in the drawing-room, I'll have no sulks from you, miss!'

Unwillingly, Prue changed her dress for a gown of flowered sarcenet with a triple fall of lace from the elbow sleeves. The high colour her mother had remarked upon was gone, and there were shadows under her eyes. Her lips tightened as she regarded herself in the mirror.

'A fine washed-out miss you look, dear Mistress Prue! No doubt but *he* would find amusement in your wan looks!' She snatched up her rouge pot and delicately smoothed a faint flush on her cheeks, and stood back to assess the result. ''Tis an improvement,' she murmured, then turned away abruptly. Why was she bothering herself? *He* would not be coming; even *his* arrogance would not allow it.

When she entered the drawing-room she found her sisters hanging out of the window, and told them sharply to pull their heads in and not make a spectacle of themselves.

''Pon honour, Prue,' Cassie exclaimed, 'you've become a fine prude these days. Pray, who are you to teach us genteel manners?'

'Who indeed!' Selina snapped waspishly. 'You should look to your own behaviour, sister, before taking it upon yourself to scold!'

'What do you mean?' Prue asked quickly, but Selina only tossed her head and muttered something about worse things than taking a look from a window, and at that moment Lady Angel sailed in, wearing her best cap with lace flaps and carrying her vinaigrette in one hand and her fan in the other.

'I declare I'm as limp as a rag! La, how an evening's entertainment does drain one's energy. But I have made acquaintance with some most genteel people, and we shall not have to depend on Dorcas for society.'

She sank on to a divan and fanned herself languidly. 'What could have made those girls of hers choose yellow and orange for their gowns? I did not consider they had the least degree of modishness, and as for Dorcas's head. . . . Such a top-heavy affair, with all those garlands and feathers——' she broke off as the door opened and the footman announced Mrs Beauford and her daughters.

'Dearest Dorcas,' Lady Angel extended a languid hand, 'how charming of you to trouble yourself to visit. Pray excuse my rising, I'm quite exhausted after last night's ball.'

''Tis but natural,' her dearest friend replied, seating herself near the divan. 'You are not used to such notable entertainments. It is quite in the order of things for us, of course.'

The Misses Beauford joined the three Angel sisters at the window.

'I expect you were all perfectly overwhelmed by the magnitude of last night's entertainment,' Caro observed, her pale eyes raking Prue's becoming gown and her dark curls held in place with a rose ribbon. 'I was quite prostrated after dancing so much. I believe you did not enjoy overmany dances? Of course we have *so* many acquaintances in society.'

'We met some friends last night,' Selina said, peering out of the window. 'I see one stepping from his carriage now.'

Prue felt her pulse leap. She stood, pretending to listen to Caro's prattle about the ball, determinedly keeping her eyes from the door. How dare he come! Was it to insult her further? Certainly it was not to apologise, that was not the way of His Grace, the Duke of Carlington!

The footman announced: 'Sir Joseph Meryton,' and Selina ran forward eagerly.

'Oh, Sir Joseph! I vow I did not believe you when you said you would not be able to keep away!' She laughed up into his face, her eyes sparkling as she made him a curtsey.

'Selina, such manners!' her mother called. 'Sir Joseph, this is vastly kind of you. Dorcas, may I present Sir Joseph Meryton.'

Prue let out the breath she had been holding in a long sigh of relief—or could it be disappointment? The snub she had prepared must be put away for another day. Not that she wished ever to see him again, but if she was forced to by her mother's overweening social ambition, she would be prepared.

More people arrived. The footman brought refreshments, sherry, madeira, ratafia, cake and biscuits, and Prue busied herself attending to their guests' wants. Suddenly, as she was pouring herself a trifle of ratafia, she found John Hillier beside her. Startled, she looked up, her colour rising.

'I wished to know how you—and your sisters—fared after the ball,' he said, bowing. 'I trust you took no harm from the night air after the heat of the ballroom?'

She assured him that they had returned in good order, and offered him a glass of sherry, then, lowering her voice, asked anxiously,

'Pray tell me at once, did the Duke dismiss you for . . . what you did last night?'

He shrugged his shoulders. 'No. I got a fine raking-down and was told I was near to losing my position, but I am to be forgiven, it appears.'

'Oh, I'm so glad. I think I have to thank you for taking such a risk for me, Mr Hillier.'

He looked at her intently for a moment before saying, 'Mistress Prue, I would gladly do the same again. Forgive me—but may I offer you a word of warning?'

She shook her head. ''Tis not needed, sir. I have had my lesson. But I thank you sincerely for your consideration.'

His gaze quickened and he said, as if the words would not be held back, 'It is more than consideration, Mistress Prue! I . . . I am at your service at any time.'

'Even if you are dismissed the Duke's service?' she asked, smiling faintly.

'It would not weigh with me for a minute.'

She touched his hand lightly. 'Sir, I am grateful. I know I have a true friend in you.'

'A friend?' His brows rose, then he sighed. 'So be it. A friend—for life.'

When the greater part of the visitors had left, Prue joined her sisters and the Beauford girls, who were eating cake and discussing the ball.

'La, Prue,' Selina cried, 'you have missed the choicest piece of scandal! Minnie observed something of it and Sir Joseph confirmed it. Lady Anastasia had a set-to with the Duke and left in a fine tweak! 'Tis said he's tired of her and looks elsewhere. The whole town will be talking of it this morning. Minnie was near the door and heard voices, and my lady was soon calling for her coach and looking as cat-faced as ever was!'

'Indeed, I fear the lady has never been able to control her

emotions in public,' Sir Joseph, who had joined them, observed, smiling. 'It gave a pleasant piquancy to the evening.'

Prue was silent as she took in this new aspect of the Duke's behaviour. It was possible that, unwittingly, *she* had been the cause of the jealous exhibition and final rift. Not that it made any difference to her opinion of him!

As a result of the ball people called, and had to be called upon. Lady Angel rejoiced, and took special care to pursue friendship with families whose sons would inherit comfortable fortunes and, possibly, titles.

The Duke, however, did not appear, much to her disappointment. Prue had met John Hillier while driving in the park, and he had told her that the Duke was out of town, and she wondered if this was the result of gossip about his split with Lady Anastasia. However, she rather thought such gossip would be unimportant to him. The Duke of Carlington was above gossip; no scandal could tumble him from his place in society. He was allowed scandals where another man would be ostracised.

One morning Prue noticed Selina lingering in the hall, looking faintly secretive. She answered pettishly when Prue spoke to her and turned away to speak to the under-footman. Prue thought no more of it, but a little later she caught sight of Selina running up the stairs to her room clutching something to her bosom, her eyes very bright and wary.

'Do you have a letter?' she asked. 'It is early, surely, for the post?'

'Oh . . . 'tis nothing of importance. A note from Minnie Beauford about some embroidery silks I wanted.'

Prue looked at her hard. 'Strange. I met Minnie this morning, and she said she would write about the silks tomorrow as she was busy today.'

'Well, she's changed her mind,' Selina said sharply. 'Anyway, 'tis not your affair.'

'I think it may be our mother's affair, Selina. I do not believe that note was from Minnie . . . I can easily ask her, you know, when we meet at dinner today. It is from a man, and I believe I know him.'

Tell-tale scarlet flooded Selina's face.

'You are the shabbiest creature! I'll not have you interfering . . .'

'It is from Sir Joseph, is it not?'

'What if it is?' Selina tossed her curls. 'He wishes me to have the—the name of a book, that is all.'

'Selina, you are a bird-witted innocent. A married man has no right to send notes to a young girl he has just become acquainted with.'

'Indeed, we are well acquainted. . . .' Selina stopped abruptly and turned her back.

'You have not been meeting him?' Prue demanded.

'Of course not! Do not be such a poker! I refuse to be bullied!'

'I wish only to warn you that you may be behaving in a most unwise manner. Your reputation——'

Selina swung round, her face puckered in a vindictive scowl.

'And pray who are you to speak of reputations? No doubt you and the Duke were discussing the beauty of the stars when you were with him in the gardens on the night of the ball . . . I saw you by the merest chance! Now who is bird-witted not to know how such behaviour could be construed?'

'I—I walked with him a few minutes; the ballroom had heated me. . . .'

'Oh, no doubt! *I* shall not question your motives—or his. And I shan't tell anyone . . . unless you continue to scold me about Sir Joseph.'

Prue swallowed her anger. 'Very well, if you will assure me there is nothing improper in your association, and promise me not to meet him on the sly.'

'Oh I'll promise,' Selina said lightly. 'Mama keeps too sharp an eye on me for anything like that.'

It was some days later that Selina received another letter, this time by the post.

'Lud, Jim West sees fit to write me a most clumsily-worded letter,' she declared, 'all about his cows and horses and how well he does at the farmers' show.' She tossed the letter aside. 'Poor Jim, he was for ever dangling after me.'

'Oh, a boorish creature,' Lady Angel said. ''Tis impertinent of him to write to you. Let him keep his letters for a dairymaid.'

'Does he speak of Papa?' Prue asked eagerly, looking up from her tapestry work.

'He says he visited him and found him in good health,' Selina said carelessly. 'Mama, did you not say that the Beaufords have a cousin visiting them?'

'Yes, a young man called Richard Unwin. His father has a good estate, and Dorcas has ideas of him for Minnie. We shall meet him tonight when we dine there.'

The dinner-party at the Beaufords was as dull as Prue expected. Mr Richard Unwin proved a sad disappointment, a prim, self-opinionated young man with a heavy manner. Minnie scowled as he bowed low and showered compliments upon the Misses Angel and their toilettes.

'Angels indeed!' he exclaimed, clasping a hand to his bosom and gazing upwards. 'Blessed with beauty and heavenly raiment!'

'My raiment did not come from heaven, I assure you,' Prue told him, 'unless heaven has opened an establishment in Bond Street.'

After the meal, Mrs Beauford said: 'I have invited a few guests in later to take tea with us and play a game of brag. Sir Joseph Meryton was gracious enough to accept.'

Instinctively Prue glanced at Selina, and saw her gratified

smile. Was it chance, or had Sir Joseph insinuated himself into the party to meet Selina?

'Does Sir Joseph's wife come with him, ma'am?' she asked Mrs Beauford.

'No, she does not go into society.'

'She was at the ball,' Cassie remarked.

'Only because she plagued him so,' Selina began, then turned, her face suddenly pink, and pretended an interest in a table of silver ornaments.

Alerted now, Prue observed Sir Joseph more closely. He was a handsome man with a charm that, she guessed, would appeal to many women. That he appealed to her sister was evident. Selina stayed beside him, insisted he partner her at cards and whispered to him behind her fan. Caro giggled, and exchanged meaning glances with Minnie.

'I ought to warn Mama,' Prue thought as she watched them, 'yet if I do, Selina will certainly let out having seen me with the Duke, and Mama will want to know why I never mentioned it. She will either disapprove, or approve all too well and think I'm in the way of catching him as a husband. If she but knew the truth! I must keep watch upon Selina myself and prevent the silly goose from losing her heart, as she thinks, to a married man who might be tempted by her obvious partiality.'

She sighed without knowing it and heard someone say,

'So deep a sigh and wistful expression! May I be allowed to try to restore your spirits, Mistress Prue?'

She looked up with a smile. 'I'faith, I feel them rising already, Mr Hillier. Come sit with me and tell me the latest scandal of the modish world.'

He returned her smile as he sat down. She was surprised at her pleasure in seeing him, and the sudden lifting of her heart.

'Are you now a devotee of the ball, Mistress Prue?' he asked.

'By no means, sir, they are vastly overrated events. I have but now recovered my energies.'

'But you have an inexhaustible supply, I think. You have a vitality that makes you sparkle and stand out from other women.'

'Your compliments have completed the treatment, sir,' she told him gaily, 'my sighs have quite vanished.'

He bowed, and she thought how much she liked him. He was a man to trust, and it was obvious that he admired her, and the knowledge pleased her. They chatted of books, music and the theatre until Lady Angel rose.

'A most elegant evening, Dorcas, I congratulate you. Come, daughters, it grows late.' She looked at John Hillier archly. 'Are you giving yourself a holiday, Mr Hillier, while the Duke is away? Pray when does His Grace return to town?'

'Next week, Lady Angel. I have instructions to prepare the house for guests.'

'Well, I trust we shall be seeing him,' Lady Angel said. 'It is always such a delight, such an honour, to be allowed to entertain so noble a personage. Do not forget to tell him, I pray. We quite pine to see him again.'

John Hillier's face was as expressionless as his voice when he assured her he would deliver her message, but Prue, catching his swift glance, very much doubted if the Duke would ever receive it.

# CHAPTER EIGHT

LADY ANGEL had made the acquaintance of the Honourable Mrs Courtney, a well-connected lady with a large family and a husband in attendance upon their Majesties, and Prue had taken a liking to the eldest daughter, Hester. The liking was returned, and the two girls found occasions to meet and go shopping, attend concerts and walk in the fashionable Mall. Hester was a quiet, intelligent girl, handsome rather than pretty, with a reserved manner that concealed a generous nature and amiable temper.

'Mama has been considering the assembly to be held in the new Pantheon in Oxford Street,' Hester remarked one morning when she and the three Angel girls were strolling in Kensington Gardens, accompanied by Harry Dunstan and Hester's brother, Ralph, a lively young gentleman of eighteen. ''Twill be a fine occasion by all accounts, and the company most select.'

'The Master of Ceremonies, Mr Donnellan, hopes it may be so,' Ralph remarked, 'but 'tis rumoured that some of the ladies of the town plan to attend, despite his published warning.'

'They would not dare!' his sister exclaimed.

'Would they not, sister? Did not Betsy Cox dance a cotillion there on the opening night?'

'Their impudence is above all things these days!' Hester protested. 'It was not so long ago that the notorious Nancy Parsons appeared at the opera with a nobleman, and his wife sitting not a yard away.'

'But gossip has it he is tired of her, and she is now taken up by some other fine buck,' Selina chimed in. 'I should dearly like to see her.'

'Mama will give you a rare set-down if she hears you speak of such women,' Cassie told her.

'Fudge!' Selina tossed her head. 'All the *ton* speaks of them. It would make me laugh were they to invade the Pantheon and put the Master of Ceremonies in the fidgets!'

Harry Dunstan shook his head. 'I agree with Mistress Courtney, such women would not dare. They know the limits of where they may show themselves.'

'Aye, in the park and at the theatre,' Selina giggled, 'and in Mother Banks' establishment in Curzon Street!'

'Selina!' Prue turned on her sister, her anger showing in her dark eyes. 'I forbid you to speak so! Where do you learn such things, pray?'

Selina pouted, and Hester broke in to say,

'If Mama decides we are to attend the Pantheon, perhaps we may go together since I think Lady Angel has expressed an interest in the event.'

'Oh, that would be delightful!' Prue cried, her anger forgotten. 'Let us implore our worthy mamas to make it a plan.'

As a group of horsemen rode past, a rider broke away and cantered up to Prue. It was John Hillier, riding a fine bay. He swung himself down to greet the company and Prue, who loved horses, went to stroke the silky neck of his mount.

John asked her if she had considered hiring a horse to ride in the park and she told him that her mother had given her consent and it was now only a matter of a new habit and a reliable mount.

'I should be greatly honoured if you will allow me to accompany you sometimes,' he said, looking down at her as she stood beside him, her cheeks delicately flushed and her dark eyes glowing as she petted the handsome bay. She was wearing a striped poplin with a cherry petticoat, and a frivolous little straw hat was perched on her glossy curls. She looked up and caught his ardent gaze, and smiled demurely.

'Indeed, I should be most grateful for your company, Mr Hillier, since I have only ridden over fields and moors at home. I shall have to learn London ways.'

'You need to learn nothing,' his voice was vehement, '*you* can teach London much, Mistress Prue.'

'Here comes our chaise,' Cassie cried, 'and Lawson signals us.'

The old coachman descended and bobbed to Prue. 'M'lady says there's company at home awaiting you, and she'll take it kindly if you'll return with me, Miss Prue.'

'I wager she said "tell them to come back at once",' Cassie groaned. 'I'd liefer continue our walk.'

'There'll be a fine kick-up if you don't oblige her ladyship,' Lawson assured her, 'with her being in a twittery state at you being away so long, miss.'

'I fear we must return,' Prue said. 'I am sorry to break up our pleasant morning, Hester.' She turned to Lawson. 'Who comes? Do you know?'

'Mrs Beauford's carriage be at the door, Miss Prue, and Lizzie tells me Sir Joseph Meryton is come.'

'Sir Joseph? Oh, let us return at once,' Selina cried, and scrambled into the chaise in such haste that she tore the frill of her gown. 'Come, Prue, Cassie, or the company will be gone!'

'I could wish Sir Joseph to be gone,' Prue whispered to Hester who nodded and murmured,

'I'm afraid your sister is a little . . . unwise. She is young, of course, and——'

'And with as much sense as a peahen,' Prue sighed, and followed her sister into the chaise.

They found the Beauford family and their cousin, Mr Richard Unwin, and Sir Joseph ensconced in the drawing-room.

'Walking in the park so early?' Caro remarked. ''Tis not fashionable at this hour, you know. And the Mall is where the *ton* meet.'

'Well, Kensington Gardens is where *we* meet,' Prue said gaily. 'How are you enjoying your visit to London, Mr Unwin?'

Mr Unwin was only too willing to give his opinion of the capital and its attractions—and pitfalls. He enlarged upon his reactions to the world of fashion while Prue let her mind wander.

*Had* she expected to hear that the Duke had at last called upon them? But of course he would not! She had made it plain that his attentions were repugnant to her, and he would not waste his time on her when he could use it with greater profit elsewhere.

From John Hillier she had learned the Duke had returned to his fine house in Cavendish Street and was entertaining visitors he had brought with him from Dorset. John had once mentioned the estate, a very splendid one with a magnificent Elizabethan mansion surrounded with great woods, a fine park and extensively cultivated gardens. Much of his land was agricultural, and contained twenty villages, the inhabitants of which worked for the Duke. Somewhat to her surprise, she learned his Grace was considered a generous landlord, and his people were well-housed and better treated than on many other estates in the county. She had not supposed he could be generous, or thoughtful of any condition but his own.

'But well-treated men will work better for him,' she thought, keeping an expression of interest on her face so that Richard Unwin should not know she had ceased listening, 'which is his reason, of course.'

She came out of her musings to hear her mother saying,

'Indeed, my sweet Dorcas, you need not feel sorry you cannot fit us into your party for the Pantheon, since we are to attend it with Mrs Courtney and her family. Mr Courtney will be with us if his court duties allow him.'

'Mama, is it settled we attend the assembly?' Prue exclaimed.

'Oh, joy!' Cassie clapped her hands. 'We must have new gowns!'

The entry of more visitors prevented further discussion. Refreshments were brought and dispensed, and the talk was all of routs and soirées and losses at White's, and the vicissitudes of the marriage of the Dauphin to the charming Marie Antoinette of Austria.

Lady Angel agreed that new gowns for so special an occasion were imperative, and visits to Bruton Street necessary for anxious consultation with a dressmaker. Lady Angel had decided upon midnight blue brocaded satin, Prue having weaned her away from a fancy for heliotrope trimmed with green. The twins, after days of agony, chose the shorter version of the polonaise, primrose for Cassie and green for Selina, with trains gathered up with braids over a flowered petticoat.

Prue's gown, a deep, glowing ruby brocade, had a triple fall of delicate lace at the sleeves and a *décolletage* edged with ruched cream velvet ribbon and tiny pearl drops. She knew the colour brought out the beauty of her eyes and complexion, and the tiny band of lace, fastened with a rosebud, would draw attention to the snowy perfection of her throat.

Interest in the assembly at the new Pantheon was growing, and the modish world was preparing for an occasion of brilliance. The Angels and the Courtneys were to meet in the hall and sit together, giving Lady Angel opportunity to question Mr Courtney about the Royal receptions at Court. Prue was happy not to be under the grudging patronage of the Beaufords, and to be with her friend, Hester.

Discreet questioning of John Hillier had revealed that the Duke of Carlington did not plan to attend the function. Not,

Prue assured herself, that it had any significance for her. He was reported as being seen with a pretty little widow of a baronet, and had obviously lost all interest in someone who had rejected his advances.

The night of the assembly came at last. Lizzie, and Mollie—the little maid Lady Angel had engaged to be her daughters' dresser—rushed to and fro, pinning, hooking up, lacing, fetching rosewater, eau de Cologne and virgin milk, finding fans, kerchiefs, reticules, polishing shoe-buckles, smoothing silk stockings, and assisting Monsieur Charles who had come to dress the heads of the ladies.

Prue insisted on a simple style with only a light dusting of powder and a tiny garland of deep red roses, but the twins emerged with elaborately puffed creations sprouting ribbons, feathers and pom-poms.

Lawson had difficulty in driving through the crowds that collected in Oxford Street to see the notabilities arrive. Groans and cat-calls greeted the coach of the unpopular Duke of Cumberland and there were only a few cheers for Lord North, plump and smiling in his very splendid carriage, reminding Prue of her father's stricture on his political ability.

At last they managed to reach the entrance and alight. The Courtneys awaited them, and together they made their way slowly through the brilliant throng to a great room domed like some Byzantine cathedral. Slender columns marked the double-sided aisles where niches held classical statues. The great dome was softly illuminated by light thrown up from gilt vases. Prue caught her breath in admiration and delight as she followed her mother and Mrs Courtney. All around she saw famous beauties, stately matrons, and gorgeous gentlemen in satin and brocade, their grandeur rivalling that of the beauties they escorted.

She was too intent upon enjoying the scene to be aware of the notice she was exciting among some of the crowd. Many a dashing buck turned from his lady to stare through his quizzing-glass at Prue's softly flushed face, liquid dark eyes shadowed with long silky lashes, and slender, graceful figure. Some of the beauties looked, too, and were not overpleased with the slim figure in glowing ruby brocade whose piquant face held something more arresting, more enchanting, than mere beauty.

They met the Beauforts who greeted them effusively and swept on. When the music struck up, Ralph Courtney came up to ask Prue to dance with him, and together they made their way into the centre of the room.

'You quite outshine all the other women, Mistress Prue,' the boy declared, aware of and enjoying the envious glances thrown at him by the men around him.

''Tis vastly kind of you to say so, sir,' Prue said, smiling at him as they paraded in the dance, 'but you are mistaken. There are many of London's proudest beauties here tonight, and you know very well that they outshine me.'

'You are quite out,' he protested, 'they pale before you. Will you dance with me again later?'

She laughed and promised she would. When they returned to their party she found that John Hillier had joined them. He caught her eye and moved towards her and began, in a low, hurried voice, 'Mistress Prue, I feel I must tell you——' but Cassie seized his arm, declaring that it was their dance and she would positively wait no longer, and dragged him away before he could finish his remark.

'No doubt he wished to claim you for a dance,' Hester said, smiling, 'but your sister captured him. However you will have no lack of partners tonight, Prue. How well that gown suits you, you are like a lovely flame, so alive and sparkling.'

She spoke the truth. Men bowed before Prue and begged a dance, and sighed if they found her already engaged. At last she had become aware of the stir she was creating, and the knowledge rose to her head like wine. To be admired, complimented, sought after! It was a sweet triumph because she had not expected it would ever happen to her. Because of the press of suitors around her, John Hillier had not been able to approach. Harry, too, was on the outside of the throng, somewhat to Cassie's relief.

Ralph came up to claim his second dance. He was slightly flushed with wine and inclined to be boastful, to Prue's amusement.

'I have danced every dance, Mistress Prue! Not a hand refused me, and several bucks quite put out of countenance, I swear! 'Tis the finest entertainment! A bang-up affair, is it not?'

'Indeed, it is very delightful,' she agreed, steadying him as they made a quick turn in the dance, 'though possibly there is somewhat too great a crowd . . .'

She turned her head sharply, hearing voices raised in sudden anger behind her. She was near the main doorway in which a man with a pretty, bold-faced young woman on his arm was standing. Before them stood Mr Donnellan, Master of Ceremonies, his hand upraised. The dance was coming to an end and couples were moving off the dance floor. Prue, instinct warning her, caught her partner's arm.

'Come away, pray do, sir.'

'I defy you to refuse us admittance!' the man in the doorway shouted furiously.

'I do not refuse you, Captain Alford,' Mr Donnellan said, 'only your . . . female companion.'

''Fore God, she'll enter and dance to her heart's delight! Eh, Sophia sweetheart?' He turned to the girl on his arm, who tossed her head and laughed shrilly.

'Stap me, 'tis the fair Sophia herself!' someone near Prue whispered.

The Master of Ceremonies was speaking. 'You are aware, Captain, that ladies of the town are not to be admitted to the entertainment. I must request you to take her away.'

'To the devil with you, damn you!' the man shouted belligerently. 'She's good enough! If you refuse every woman who's a wanton, you'll have an empty room! What's to differ between Sophia and ... and ...' before she realised his intention, the man, his heavy face suffused with fury, had stepped forward and seized Prue's wrist, dragging her towards his companion, '... and this pretty nymph?'

'Damn you, sirrah! Unhand her this minute!' It was Ralph's voice, high-pitched and furious. He rushed forward. 'I'll make you pay for this insult!'

'Gentlemen! Gentlemen!' Mr Donnellan pleaded. 'There must be no violence! I beg you to remember——'

'You young puppy!' the captain howled. 'I'll fight you into hell!' Light gleamed wickedly on the sword he had drawn, and a gasp of dismay arose from the little group of watchers. The majority of the company had left the ballroom in search of refreshment, and were as yet unaware of the situation.

Prue stood perfectly still, all colour draining from her face. She heard the girl whisper, 'Lawks, Alford, he's but a baby! Leave him alone.'

'He'll fight me, by God—or be branded as a coward.'

Ralph's young face was suddenly aflame. He took a quick step forward, but as he raised his hand to strike his opponent, his arm was caught and a cool voice said, 'You were ever quarrelsome in your cups, Alford. Sheathe your weapon this instant.'

Prue gasped, her hand flying to her heart as she gazed dumbfounded at the tall, Olympian figure of His Grace, the Duke of Carlington.

# CHAPTER NINE

'LET me free!' Ralph choked. 'I'll fight him! Let him choose the time and place!'

'I think not.' Without quite knowing how, Ralph found himself edged back among the silent watchers while His Grace the Duke of Carlington turned to the agitated Mr Donnellan and said in a low voice. 'Let the lady enter, sir. This display of drunken bravado is not to my liking.'

Mr Donnellan looked at him for a moment, then bowed silently and stepped aside. Mistress Sophia swept forward, an impudent smile upon her full lips, and paused for a second to whisper to Prue: 'Lud, the poor fellow's bosky! He meant you no harm, miss,' before moving through the group, leaving a trail of whispers and stifled laughter behind her.

Her incensed escort made no attempt to follow her. He stared past the Duke to where Ralph, abruptly sobered and white-faced, stood uncertainly.

'Out of my way, Your Grace! I'll settle where to meet that young swaggerer tomorrow morning!'

'Oh no, indeed you must not!' Prue, suddenly alive to the situation, moved forward hastily. 'You provoked him. . . .'

'You forget something,' the Duke's eyes were on the angry man trying to push past him. He did not glance once in Prue's direction. 'You will have to settle with me first.'

'You?' The Captain stared. 'I . . . I don't understand; I've nothing to settle with Your Grace, 'tis that young cockerel whose throat I'll split! I've no wish to offend you——'

'But you have, my dear Alford. I fear I have taken exception to your behaviour.' The Duke spoke coldly. 'But if you choose to apologise. . . .'

'I . . . of course, Your Grace! I had no intention to——'

'Naturally you had not,' the Duke said smoothly, 'because you are distressingly foxed, my dear Alford—and so is our young friend here. And there can be no duels set up between drunken men. Go, find your partner and let us hear no more of this paltry business.'

He turned with lazy grace and offered Prue his arm. As in a daze, she took it and together they crossed the ballroom and entered the refreshment room where the crowds were busy finding places for themselves and their partners amid a babble of chatter and laughter.

Still badly shaken, she managed to whisper, 'Your Grace, I am grateful——'

'No word,' he said sternly, 'until I have found a seat and brought you a glass of wine.'

In some miraculous way he found her a seat in a secluded corner, away from the crowd. While she awaited his return, she tried to control her quivering nerves and regain some poise. The episode, with poor Ralph's rushing to defend her, had shaken her, but it was nothing to the surge of emotion she had felt when she saw the Duke. Why was he here? John had said he did not plan to attend the assembly . . . Suddenly she remembered John's attempt to tell her something before Cassie had pulled him away. Of course! He had wanted to warn her the Duke had changed his mind.

'Drink this.' He was standing before her, holding out a glass of wine.

'I—I would prefer some lemonade——'

'I said drink this,' he commanded, and automatically she took the glass and drank, and felt a measure of strength and composure return.

He pulled up a chair and seated himself beside her.

'I have told the waiter to bring us supper. I do not intend to do battle at the table.'

'But I must find my mother, she will be wondering where I am.'

'There is no possibility of finding anyone in this crush,' he said calmly. 'When we have supped, you shall seek her. You are not in a condition to brave this crowd, Mistress Prue. You are very pale.'

'I was excessively frightened,' she admitted. 'I feared poor Ralph would perhaps be embroiled in a—in a duel!' She looked at him, her eyes anxious. 'Is it possible Captain Alford will call him out? Ralph is but eighteen, 'twould be abominable.'

'He is safe,' he said, as two waiters hurried up to set a small table before them with wine and food. 'Alford was foxed. But I shall drop a hint to Courtney that a short absence from London might be expedient for Master Ralph. The intemperate captain will be recalled to his regiment.'

'How can you be sure?' Prue demanded.

A smile touched his well-cut mouth. 'Such things can be . . . arranged. Now oblige me by eating some of these oyster patties and getting colour back into your cheeks.'

Prue hesitated, looking around the room, but there was no sign of any of her party, and she was aware that she was hungry! There would be little sense in refusing to stay and eat supper with His Grace the Duke.

'A wise decision,' the Duke murmured, amusement in his eyes as he watched her. 'You are safe here; I shall not attempt to abduct you under the eyes of the world, I assure you.' His gaze grew intent as he went on softly: 'But the notion is an intriguing one, Mistress Prue. You are unversed in love, but a man might find heaven in teaching you.'

She looked up, her eyes flashing in sudden anger.

'My lord Duke, I am here because I cannot find my family, but I shall not remain if you continue to speak so to me!

You have insulted me once, and I do not mean you to do so again. 'Twere better I became lost in the crowd than listen to you!'

He bowed, his grey eyes mocking, and filled his glass with wine.

He remained silent for a time while she ate. Prue kept her eyes upon the glittering crowd around the long table laden with every expensive luxury, but she was aware of him in every nerve of her body. She was deeply dismayed that he should affect her so, but there was little she could do about it. He was dangerous, he had power and he knew how to use it. But now she knew her danger she would fight it!

Her weakness was only momentary. The scene she had witnessed and her fears for Ralph had put her in a fluster, and she had not yet perfectly recovered. She would never let him know that he had the power to discompose her.

Suddenly she caught sight of Cassie with Harry. They were looking around, searching for her. She rose abruptly.

'I see my sister and shall join her. I am grateful to you for your assistance in a most distasteful incident.' She curtsied and turned swiftly before he could speak.

'Why, Prue, where have you hidden yourself?' Cassie demanded. 'Harry and I have looked for you.'

'I heard something of a brawl at the door,' Harry said, looking at her anxiously. 'I trust there was nothing to distress you?'

'Oh, nothing much,' she said lightly. 'A drunken captain saw fit to make a noise. The Duke of Carlington rescued me.' It was best to admit meeting him, since someone else might remark upon it. 'Where are Mama and Mrs Courtney?'

The two matrons had found a corner of the table and were enjoying their supper. When Cassie revealed that the Duke was present, Lady Angel ceased nibbling a preserved pear to exclaim, 'His Grace here? Oh! we must seek him out! I shall remind him that he has positively forgotten us these last weeks.'

'I am positive he has left,' Prue said quickly, 'he found the crowd too great.'

Later, when she got Hester alone, she told her friend of her unpleasant experience.

Hester exclaimed in dismay. 'Dearest Prue, how distressing for you! Poor Ralph is sadly headstrong!'

'He is brave, he wished to avenge an insult to me.'

'I am glad he did so. But if this Captain Alford should remember the episode, and perhaps seek revenge——'

'There is no danger,' Prue hastened to assure her. 'But I think the Duke means to suggest to your father that Ralph should leave London until the Captain is recalled.'

'It is kind of His Grace to think of it,' Hester said warmly. 'I admit I have not cared for what I hear of his reputation, but he has behaved with consideration this evening.'

To Lady Angel's annoyance she was unable to discover the Duke, and Prue had to endure a scolding in the coach on the way home because she had neither brought him into her party nor invited him to Grosvenor Street. They had met John Hillier for a moment on the way out, and he had whispered to Prue,

'I sought to tell you the Duke was present after all. Is it true that you encountered him?'

Swiftly she gave him an account of what had happened.

'I must be grateful to His Grace. Poor Ralph might otherwise be in a scrape.'

John frowned. 'Did the Duke know you were to be here tonight?'

'I do not see how he could have known,' she told him.

'Prue, pray hasten or we shall miss our coach,' Lady Angel broke in. She saw John and smiled graciously. 'Mr Hillier, I have not had the honour of meeting His Grace in such a press, but inform him I tried, and am excessively disappointed.'

John bowed, and moved aside to let them past.

Selina had been too absorbed with Sir Joseph, who had appeared shortly after their arrival, to know of any disturbance in the evening; but Cassie had heard something of it and began to speak of it but, catching Prue's warning eye, subsided, yawning.

'I vow I'm vastly sleepy all of a sudden. But 'twas an excessively pleasant evening, and I consider my gown as elegant as any there. Harry certainly thought so.'

Prue smiled at her. 'You looked most charming, and I suspect that Harry was not your only admirer.'

'*I* could have danced every dance had I chosen,' Selina, who had been gazing dreamily out of the window, remarked.

'I did not observe you dancing much, Selina,' her mother said. 'Where were you?'

'Oh, it got so hot and airless in that big room; I preferred conversation in a quieter and cooler place.'

'With Sir Joseph.' Cassie sat up. 'Sister, you are a goose-head! You flirt too much. He is a married man, do not forget it.'

'Oh, fudge! You're jealous because I have attached a man of title and not a penny-pincher in the law courts like poor Harry!'

'No more of this naughty cat-scrapping,' Lady Angel ordered. 'But Cassie is right, Selina. You will get yourself talked about if you display such partiality for Sir Joseph. He is a man of high purpose, I've no doubt, and does not wish to hurt your feelings by giving you the set-down you deserve. It is better you do not meet him so often.'

Selina went scarlet, then white, and sank back in her corner of the coach and spoke no more. Prue felt relieved that her mother had at last realised Selina's reckless behaviour, and hoped it would be the end of the matter. But a glance at her sister's brooding face made her uneasy, and she decided to keep an unobtrusive watch upon her.

Next day Mrs Courtney and her daughters called to discuss the assembly. Hester drew Prue into a corner.

'There is some mention of last night's upset in the *Morning Post*, Prue, but your name is not mentioned, I'm pleased to report.'

'That pleases me also,' Prue assured her.

'The Captain was altogether in the wrong; he attempted to force a woman of no character into the assembly.'

'He was also drunk. How is Ralph feeling about it?'

'He has decided to visit his uncle in Devonshire,' Hester said. 'It is a wise move. The Duke was vastly tactful.'

'You have met him?' Prue asked in some surprise.

'I observed him while he spoke to my parents. He is a fine figure of a man, is he not? No doubt he will be calling on you to see how you do after last night.'

Involuntarily Prue's eyes went to the door. She was grateful to the Duke, but she did not wish to meet him again. In time, she would master the agitation he aroused in her. Last night he had saved her from an awkward situation and Ralph from a possible duel, and for that she was grateful. But she would never trust him, or believe in his protestation of love. Such a man did not know the meaning of love. It was the chase, the capture, the surrender that excited his lust. Did not his reputation bear it out?

Hester was speaking. 'Mr Hillier, the Duke's secretary, is a pleasant, well-conducted young man, I find.'

'Yes indeed,' Prue agreed, glad to have her thoughts directed elsewhere. Her heart warmed as she thought of John's eyes seeking hers, and the concern in his face when they last met. Here was a man who asked nothing, who treated her with respect, and who had been the means of rescuing her from the Duke's embrace at the St James's

Square ball; and who, she suspected, was falling in love with her.

Selina was subdued for some days, refusing to take part in walks in the park, shopping or visiting. She answered sulkily when spoken to and at last her mother's patience gave out.

'You're as sour as a lemon, Selina! Moping about with a mum-face! I'll have no more of this nonsense. Go out with your sisters and get some fresh air to cure your sallow looks!'

'I need some lace to trim a cap,' Selina said abruptly. 'I'll take Molly with me, she don't mind waiting. A footman fidgets me. I will not join Prue and Cassie, they waste time chattering.'

'Very well, and see that you come back without your sulks.'

As the days passed and there was no sign of a visit from the Duke, Lady Angel grew peevish under her dear Dorcas's insinuations that His Grace had tired of them and looked elsewhere for amusement. John did not visit either, and she had no way of sending obsequious reminders to His Grace of the hearty welcome awaiting him at Grosvenor Street.

''Twas vastly thoughtless of you not to have invited the Duke to the house when you met him at the Pantheon,' she reproached Prue as they drove in the chaise to take tea with the Beaufords. The twins had spent the afternoon shopping with Caro and Minnie, and were already at the Beauford house awaiting them. 'Such an opportunity, after he had condescended to extract you from such an unmannerly brawl! In pure gratitude it was your *duty* to invite him.'

'It was not my place to invite him, Mama,' Prue said firmly. 'He is a man far above us, his rank prevents our ever becoming intimate.'

'He has an interest in you, I think.'

Prue looked swiftly at her mother, struck by something in her voice. Lady Angel did not meet her eyes, but fiddled restlessly with the reticule hanging from her waist.

'Mama, surely you know that—*interest* from such a man is near to an insult?'

'Fustian! You grow strangely missish these days! If the Duke sees fit to admire you, you must take advantage of it. 'Twould be the barest folly and positive wickedness not to do so.'

Prue felt a chill creep over her as she studied her mother's face. Usually either complacent or peevish, it now bore an expression that disturbed her. Truly Lady Angel had taken up the ways and the double standards of modish society! There was a hardness about her mouth and a calculating look in her eyes when she at last raised them to meet Prue's gaze.

'You will be a fool, daughter, if you do not see the advantage that lies before you.'

'Ma'am, do you know what you imply?' Prue felt the hot blood surge into her cheeks. 'Would you have me entice the Duke to take me up as his latest whim? To draw the eyes of the world upon me as his . . . mistress?' It was time to speak bluntly.

'Fie upon you for a goose, miss! I said nothing about such a thing! He would never suggest anything shameful or——'

'Pardon me, ma'am, he most certainly would,' Prue assured her sternly.

'Fudge!' Her mother's eyes raked her suddenly. 'Do you mean . . . Has he. . . .'

'I mean nothing. I have no interest in the Duke, nor he in me.'

For a moment her mother said nothing. Then, her eyes on Prue's heated face, she said slowly, 'Do not pretend innocence, daughter. You must know perfectly well that such a man can be . . . persuaded into marriage eventually. Such an alliance would be very fine for you.'

'It would be impossible!' Prue burst out, her eyes fiery. 'You amaze me, ma'am! I had not realised how—how imbued you had become with the ambitions and wiles of London society!'

'How dare you speak so to me! You are highly impertinent! Hold your tongue, miss, I am vastly displeased with you!' Lady Angel's face quivered in indignation. She turned her head, and they remained silent until the chaise drew up before the Beauford residence.

# CHAPTER TEN

HESTER glanced quickly at Prue when she entered the Beauford drawing-room, and after a few minutes drew her aside.

'Prue, my dear, you look somewhat overset. Is anything the matter?'

'I have had a quarrel with my mother,' Prue admitted. 'She was being . . . unreasonable. Can we leave the company for a moment or two?'

'Come up to the study, we shall be quiet there.'

For a moment Prue considered telling her friend what had occurred, and of her shock at discovering how worldly her mother had become, but she remained silent. She felt shame for her mother and could not share that shame, so she merely said that Lady Angel had different ideas from hers and it had occasioned high words.

Hester's gaze was a trifle too penetrating for comfort.

'There is much I dislike and distrust in society,' she said thoughtfully. 'There is a falsity, a spurious splendour, Prue, that covers decayed morals and a brittle cynicism. My own mother has not, thank God, been affected by it, but I see it in my sisters. We had best try to ignore it, my dear, and guard against it ourselves.'

Prue pressed her hand, knowing that Hester had guessed something of the truth. After a few minutes' talk on other subjects, they rejoined the company downstairs.

The first thing Prue noticed was that Selina was looking, for the first time in a week, excited and gay. She was teasing

Richard Unwin, and that serious young sprig was trying to evade her sallies. Thank goodness, Prue thought, she has got out of her grizzles. Perhaps she'll take a fancy to Mr Unwin; she'll not be in trouble there!

Mrs Beauford was complaining to Lady Angel about the difficulty of getting tickets for Almack's, that most exclusive club.

'Vouchers are needed,' she sighed, 'and a debutante has to be introduced by a member who will sponsor her.'

'Do you not know a lady from whom you can procure cards?' Lady Angel asked.

Her friend glanced slyly at her. 'We do not pretend to move in quite such noble society as you, my sweet Clarissa. No doubt his Grace the Duke of Carlington could see his way to find a sponsor if he wished.'

Lady Angel bit her lip and shot a fretful glance at Prue.

'Oh, His Grace could certainly do it, but one hesitates to make supplication.'

'Perhaps His Grace has not granted you so much of his attention of late,' her friend murmured. 'It is understandable; His Grace has other interests.'

'I should dearly like to attend Almack's!' Cassie cried. 'It would set the seal upon our position in society.' She glanced at the door, not for the first time, and asked with a careless air: 'Did you mention that Mr Harry Dunstan might be with us today, ma'am?'

'I believe so. Ah, he comes.' Mrs Beauford smiled at Harry, who advanced to bow.

Cassie sat forward on her chair, her eyes sparkling. But Harry turned to Prue, to ask how she had enjoyed her first ride in the park. She had ridden out with a groom a few mornings ago, she told him, and greatly enjoyed it. When he asked if he might ride with her some morning, she agreed with pleasure. She liked Harry; he had a steady, sensible nature and a pleasant sense of humour, and there was a sturdiness about him that appealed to her.

Cassie, overhearing, was not pleased. 'Indeed, I think you might suggest you ride with *me*, Harry. Prue is a good horsewoman, while I need some instruction.'

'Come with us,' Prue invited, 'then Harry can instruct us both.' But she saw by her sister's expression that this was not at all what was in her mind.

As she and Cassie went up the stairs to their bedrooms that night, Cassie said abruptly, 'Selina was as fine as ninepence today, was she not? Strange how she has changed from her ill-humour.'

'I am very glad she has.'

'Do you think she has been seeing Sir Joseph again?'

Prue paused, her hand on the banister rail. 'But how could she? He has not called, nor been at any entertainment we have attended. And she seldom goes out now.'

Cassie shrugged. 'Well, she is devilish headstrong, and she thinks him a perfect paragon. She would think it a high adventure to meet him slyly.'

Prue felt a stir of uneasiness. Selina had promised not to meet Sir Joseph secretly, but what was a promise to a silly, infatuated girl? Without proof, it was useless to go to her mother. Selina was Lady Angel's favourite, and no doubt she would refuse to suspect her darling of misbehaviour—until it was too late.

It was some days later, when Prue and Hester were driving home from a visit to a millinery establishment, that Prue remembered a pair of slippers she had left to be mended, and told the coachman to drive as near the shop as he could.

'The shoemaker is down a narrow alleyway,' she explained to Hester. 'I shall walk to it, it is not far.'

She was coming out of the shop with her slippers in a parcel when she saw Mollie, their little maid, standing in the alleyway. Prue stared in amazement, then a sudden suspicion made her hurry across and confront the girl.

'Mollie! What are you doing here, pray?'

If she had had any thoughts that the girl was on some innocent business, they were blown away by the open guilt and fear on her face. Mollie shrank back, her eyes wide.

'Oh, Miss Prue! I—I didn't see you!'

'I have asked you, what do you do here?'

The girl licked her lips and glanced behind her before answering, 'I . . . I had buying to do. . . .'

'You are not alone, are you?' The girl's dismayed gasp told Prue what she already suspected. 'Miss Selina is with you, is she not? *Where is she now*? If you do not tell me the truth I shall have you punished and dismissed our house!'

'Oh, Miss Prue . . . I—I know it were very wrong, but Miss Selina, she says as how she must meet someone and it were all right, only she don't wish her mother to know . . . and. . . .'

'And she paid you well to hold your tongue, isn't that true?' Prue gripped the girl's arm, shaking her sharply.

'Oh no, Miss Prue! But she give me her striped gown and a lace flounce, and. . . .' The girl's face crumpled and she began to cry. 'Oh, don't 'ee tell the mistress, Miss Prue! She'll send me off without a character and I'll starve!'

'You should have thought of that earlier,' Prue said sternly. 'If you tell me the truth I shall not punish you. Where is my sister?'

Mollie pointed a trembling finger at a door behind them.

'She . . . she meets him in there, Miss Prue.'

Prue shivered, her heart turning to ice. That Selina could be so unthinking, so mad to risk her reputation, and with a handsome debauchee who could never marry her! A step made her look up to see Selina, her face suddenly blanched, staring at her.

Prue found her voice. 'Come with me this instant, the carriage is in the next street. You may go home, Mollie.' She took her sister's arm, but Selina pulled away furiously.

'How dare you spy upon me! I shall not allow you to dictate to me! I—I have been seeing about a—a ring I wished altered.'

Prue glanced at the door and saw it had the name of a jeweller on it.

'Selina, I am not taken in by your shams. You have been meeting Sir Joseph. I shall speak to him——'

'He has gone.' Selina tossed her head, her eyes spiteful. 'You are jealous because I have an admirer and you and Cassie remain unsought! If you dare to tell Mama——'

'I shall certainly tell her!' Prue gripped her sister's arm more firmly. 'She must know. You may already have been ruined! Selina, what mad folly drove you to such a pass? You must never see this libertine again!'

Selina looked at her with a curious expression, then she shrugged and allowed herself to be led to the coach where Prue explained to Hester that she had found her sister and maid shopping, and Selina had decided to accompany them home.

Lady Angel must be told. Selina's wild behaviour could no longer remain hidden; she must be made to see her terrible danger and, hopefully, saved from its consequences. But Prue felt her heart sink at the thought of having to tell her mother, knowing that even her new-found easiness of conscience would not condone secret meetings between her daughter and a man of no honour.

She found her mother in the morning-room reading the *London Chronicle*. Prue did not mince her words. When Lady Angel had taken it in, which at first she was unable or unwilling to do, she fell back in her chair, her eyes terrified and hands clasped to her breast.

'Oh! Oh! I *cannot* believe it! No, it is not true, Selina would never . . . She is a naughty wench and teases me, but to do such a thing . . . No, 'tis impossible! You are telling farradiddles, Prue!'

'Alack, ma'am, you must believe it is true. Selina has confessed that she meets this man slyly. Perhaps it may be but a reckless flirtation, he may be flattered by her infatuation. I shall send her to you.'

Prue refused to be present at the interview, but Cassie was summoned and made to stay and hear her sister accused of disgracing herself, railed at for behaving like a wicked wanton—and finally forgiven on her promise to cast off Sir Joseph for ever. Cassie reported to Prue later.

'La, Selina put a bold face on it at first, but Mama would have none of it, and soon she was weeping like a thunder-shower. She promises she has not lost her virtue and will forget Sir Joseph.'

'Thank God she at last shows some sense,' Prue exclaimed.

Cassie looked at her, then shrugged. 'Selina can be vastly obstinate.'

'What do you mean?' Prue asked quickly, caught by something in Cassie's face. But her sister turned away, saying,

'I don't know I've any great meaning . . . except that Selina is an obstinate goose-head.'

In her letters to her father Prue had described the amusements she had attended and the places of interest she had visited, and her rides in the park and friendship with Hester Courtney. But she had said nothing of her mother's increasing social ambitions, or Selina's unfortunate infatuation. Sir Roland was too frail and elderly to be troubled, it was kinder to let him live in tranquillity and write only of such events as would interest and amuse him. She wrote of Harry Dunstan and John Hillier, but not of the Duke. She told of the assembly at the Pantheon, but not all that had happened there. She knew her mother wrote but seldom and was unlikely to tell him much beyond describing the new gowns and caps she had bought, and the latest fashion in dressing a lady's head.

Selina avoided her, and Prue knew she was not forgiven for

disclosing her flirtation to her mother. Hester noticed and remarked upon it.

'I fear there has been some difference between you; Selina looks so sourly at you. Perhaps she is put in a fidget because Sir Joseph Meryton is gone away to the country. 'Tis as well, I think.'

'Indeed, yes,' Prue agreed with a sigh. 'I trust she will get over her trickish behaviour and find some handsome young blade to amuse her.'

Selina, considering Mollie to have been party to her undoing, spoke harshly to her, and the little maid's eyes were often red and she shrank away when Selina came near. Lady Angel had been for dismissing the girl without a character, but Prue had spoken for her, pointing out that Selina had led her into duplicity and the girl was not entirely to blame. Mollie's gratitude was deep, and she was assiduous in her attentions to Prue and left Lizzie, when she could, to dress Selina.

One afternoon Lady Angel took the chaise to go visiting in the fashionable suburb of Knightsbridge, taking Cassie with her. Prue was engaged to go with the Courtney family to the studio of Sir Joshua Reynolds, near Cranbourne Alley, to admire his painting of Lady Cookburn, which was being much praised. Selina, who was to have accompanied her, complained of feeling unwell, and indeed she looked unusually flushed and her eyes were over-bright when her mother went to her room.

'I believe 'tis a light fever,' Lady Angel told her. 'A trifle of Peruvian Bark with a drop of cinnamon will set you to rights. Lizzie shall bring it to you. You must remain in bed, Selina, till the fever is gone.'

The visit to the studio delighted Prue, and she and Hester amused themselves in noting and discussing the celebrities in the modish crowd. The huge, gross figure of the famous Doctor Johnson dwarfing that of his friend, Mr Oliver Goldsmith, whose wig was sadly out of condition and who seemed in no way put out about it; Mr David Garrick, now retired from the stage, with his pretty little Viennese wife; and the sprinkling of Fair Impures with their beaux. Lady Anastasia Storrington was present, more beautiful than ever, flirting her fan at a dashing young buck reputed to be her newest lover.

Prue declined Mrs Courtney's invitation to come back with her and take some refreshment, saying that she was a little anxious about Selina and would prefer to return to Grosvenor Street. As she ascended the steps of the house, the door was opened by James, the butler, whose usually impassive face appeared disturbed.

'Is her ladyship with you, Miss Prue?'

'No, she will not return until later. Why, is aught wrong?' When he did not answer, she had a sudden presentiment of trouble. 'James, is Miss Selina worse? Has the fever increased?'

'No, Miss Prue, Miss Selina is . . . is gone out.'

Prue stared at him. 'Gone out? 'Tis impossible! My sister was unwell and in bed when I left.'

'Shortly after you had gone, Miss Prue,' James said unhappily, 'Miss Selina arose and—and left the house. William here,' he indicated the young footman, 'saw her slip out and told me at once, but. . . .'

Prue swung round. 'Where is Mollie? Send her to me!'

The girl came forward, her face tear-stained and white.

'Oh, miss, 'twas none of my doing, as God's my witness! I never saw her go, but when William said as he'd seen her and thought he heard a coach——'

'A coach?' Prue gasped, icy fear gripping her.

'Yes, miss. I runs to her room and—and finds she's took a valise and some clothes—and her jewel-case! Seems she were in a fine hurry, leaving everything scrimble-scramble! I found this by the door, she must have dropped it. . . .'

Prue snatched the crumpled note from her, and as she read

the few lines her face blanched and James moved forward anxiously to say, 'Are you all right, Miss Prue? Take your mistress to the morning-room, girl, she's taken faint. And you, William, fetch a glass of wine.'

Prue walked unsteadily into the room and sank into a chair, shivering.

'Mollie, has my sister received any notes of late—or sent any out of the house?'

'Indeed, I've no way of knowing, miss, her being in a rage with me! 'Tis possible one of the other girls may have smuggled in something. I swear I didn't ever——'

'I know you didn't, Mollie. She has gone with him! Oh, what shall I do? What will my poor mother say? How can I stop them?'

She covered her face with her hands. Suddenly she became aware of voices in the hall. Mollie whispered, 'Laws! 'Tis a visitor!'

Then the door opened and James announced with a strong note of protest in his voice, 'His Grace the Duke of Carlington!'

# CHAPTER ELEVEN

He entered the room with a quick, firm stride and waited until the butler had shut the door behind him. Then he said sharply, 'What is this upset? Your man was in a mind to forbid me. What has happened?'

Prue had risen at the sound of his name and colour rushed into her cheeks as she struggled for composure.

'I . . . I am sorry James saw fit to. . . . But something has happened, and . . . Oh, pray forgive me, but I cannot see you now, Your Grace! Pray leave me!'

He came over to her. 'No, you are sadly upset, I can see. Where are your mother and sisters? Can I not summon them?'

'They are not here. I have been away and just returned to discover. . . .' She put her hands to her face, swaying slightly.

He took her arm. 'Sit down, you are faint.' He turned as the footman came in with a glass of wine on a salver. 'Give it to me, and send for her maid.'

'No,' Prue said quickly, 'I shall be over it in a minute. 'Tis but the effect of the shock.'

'Drink your wine, then tell me what this shock is,' he commanded. 'I shall not leave until I know your trouble.'

She looked up at him and knew he would indeed remain standing before her, with his grey eyes bent frowningly upon her, until he had the truth. A sudden weakness overtook her, and almost of their own volition the words rushed out.

'My sister Selina has flown . . . with Sir Joseph Meryton! My maid found a note.' She held it out in a trembling hand.

He took it and read, his frown deepening. Abruptly he asked, 'When did she go? Is it long since?'

'No,' she whispered, and took a sip of wine to steady her voice. 'It cannot be more than two hours. A coach was waiting.'

'He says they will make for the coast.' His Grace's face was stern, and he bit his lip as he studied the note. 'Dover, of course, since he plans to reach France. Had you known of this intrigue?'

'We knew she had a partiality for Sir Joseph, and had been—had been meeting him in secret. But she promised my mother never to see him again, and we thought....'

'You thought a feather-headed chit, infatuated with a known rake, could be trusted. Aye, 'tis often so.'

'He is a heartless monster!' Prue cried. 'To ruin her! To ruin us all and bring sorrow and shame upon us! She is but young, and as yet knows little of the wickedness of London!'

'I'faith, you can find wickedness outside London as well,' he said dryly, 'if you care to look for it. Sir Joseph has an ill reputation with women, and it is unfortunate it is not wider known. He is a heartless profligate and his wife is an unhappy, ill-used woman.' He put his hand on her shoulder as she attempted to rise. 'Rest awhile, Prue, and let us consider what may be done.'

She stared at him, her eyes wide. 'But—can anything be done? We do not know which way they travel; they may not go direct, to avert capture.'

He did not answer her. Instead, he began to pace to and fro, his face thoughtful and his mouth set in a hard line. She watched him, a sudden hope stirring in her breast. He was an impressive figure in his dark red coat with silver galoon trimming and white silk breeches. A magnificent ruby gleamed on his finger. His hair was lightly powdered and tied with a black ribbon. He swung a quizzing glass as he walked.

For the first time she wondered why he had called. Was she

glad to see him? Why had she revealed Selina's elopement? Was it because she had been unable to hide her distress, or had some instinct made her turn to his strength in this hour of horror and fear? She did not know. Yet, watching him, she felt a strange comfort, a support she sorely needed.

Abruptly he swung around. 'If the couple are apprehended and your sister restored to her mother, will she repeat her performance?'

'No. I think her father must be told and she, perhaps all of us, may return to Northumberland.'

''Twould be the best thing could you get your sister wed,' he murmured. 'London is no place for her, for sure.' He straightened his shoulders. 'If I prevent this elopement, what may I expect in return?'

Prue caught her breath. 'Is it possible you can prevent their escaping—and my sister's ruin? Our gratitude ... my mother's blessing ...'

'I want neither. What of yourself?' He came over to her and caught her hands, drawing her to her feet so that she stood before him. 'How will you look upon me if I save your sister? Will you look upon me more kindly if I save your sister? Will you, perhaps, answer my letters? Will you cease hating me, Prue, and try to ... like me a little?'

For a second the blood drummed in her ears, making her giddy.

'You would earn my heartfelt gratitude, Your Grace,' she whispered. 'I would not—I could not—hate you then.'

'But you would not try to love me, Prue.' He flung her hands away. 'I do not know why I ask; for sure, I do not intend to beg!'

He took a quick turn, then swung around and she saw his eyes were hard and mocking. 'I would give much to dismiss you from my thoughts, but since that appears to be as yet impossible ...' He walked to the door and with his hand on the handle added coldly: 'I shall see that the runaways are prevented from leaving the city. Prepare to receive your unruly sister ere long—and I advise your mother to lock her up!' He bowed slightly, and was gone.

Prue stood as if transfixed. She heard the front door shut and the rattle of wheels outside. Then all was silent except for the beating of her heart. They were saved! Shame at Selina's reckless behaviour was still there, but lasting humiliation and public disgrace would be prevented. And she had him to thank, the man she despised and wished never to see again! She did not question his ability to do what he said; His Grace the Duke of Carlington had powers denied to lesser men.

A gentle tap on the door announced James, who asked in anxious tones if she would not take some refreshment.

She managed to smile at him. 'Thank you James, perhaps I will now, the wine has given me something of an appetite.' Her mind worked swiftly. 'I have discovered that Miss Selina has gone off in a pet to stay with Mrs Courtney and her family, and the Duke knows of it and will convey a message to her to return.' She was relieved to see that the butler believed her. ''Twas naught but a family argument,' she assured him. 'My sister has a quick temper and wished to frighten us. Pray suppress any gossip among the servants.'

He bowed. 'Certainly, Miss Prue. I am much relieved. I had feared—er——' he coughed, apologetically, avoiding her glance.

'So did I, just for a moment,' she said. 'However, all is well and my sister will be home betimes.'

A tremendous load seemed to have been lifted from her, and she found she was able to enjoy a light supper of chicken salad and a syllabub. She listened for the sound of her mother's carriage and when it came, she ran into the hall.

'I vow my luck is completely out at cards,' Lady Angel said peevishly, shedding her wraps. 'I have been vastly bored! Is Selina's fever improved?'

'Come into the morning-room, Mama.' Prue urged her

mother gently towards the door. 'Selina's fever is quite gone.'

''Twas the Peruvian Bark, mark my words,' Lady Angel said, sinking on to the sofa and fanning herself. 'Cassie, go and see how your sister does.'

'Wait!' Prue held up her hand. 'Mama and Cassie, I have to tell you of something. When I returned here I found Selina had flown with Sir Joseph. She had dropped his note in her haste, and in it he directed her to be ready when he came with a carriage this evening. They planned to reach France.'

Lady Angel's face slowly blanched to a pale putty colour, and her mouth opened and shut foolishly as she stared at Prue.

Cassie gasped, then burst out: 'I suspected she was telling bouncers when she swore she had abandoned him! To deliver herself into his hands! Oh, the mad, wicked wretch!'

'No!' Lady Angel whispered. 'No, it is false! She would never . . .' Prue's glance cut her short, and with a shriek she fell back against the cushions and began drumming her heels on the floor.

Prue bent over her. 'Stop, Mama—or I shall slap you, *hard*!'

Her mother's heels stilled and she glared at Prue.

'Unfeeling chit! When your poor sister is ruined, shamed before all the world! Sir Joseph is a married man. . . . She is lost to us for ever!'

'She is *not* lost,' Prue said firmly. 'Pray listen, Mama. The Duke came——'

'The *Duke*? Oh! Our shame is indeed known! I shall never recover! Oh! Oh! Oh!' She sat up abruptly as Prue's hand came none too lightly down on her cheek. 'How *dare* you, Prue!'

'You force me,' Prue told her impatiently. 'Pray *listen*. I told the Duke all——'

'Prue!How *could* you reveal such a disgrace?'

'—and he is gone to fetch Selina back,' Prue ended calmly,

and sat down to watch the result of her words. Lady Angel was once more speechless, and Cassie's eyes were dancing.

'Oh, Prue, 'tis good beyond belief! Faith, if anyone could rescue the chicken-head, 'tis he! And he's not one to gossip. We're saved!'

'The—the Duke,' Lady Angel mumbled. ''Tis impossible. How can he . . .?'

'He knows Sir Joseph's reputation; it is not the first time, I think, that gentleman has attempted to seduce a young girl,' Prue said. 'His Grace will prevent their leaving London, they cannot have travelled far. Now, Mama, you shall take a glass of brandy and one of your tablets to soothe your nerves while we wait. Cassie, come with me.'

Outside the room, Prue showed Cassie the note Selina had dropped. Cassie nodded as she read it.

'I said she was ever mad for adventure. She thinks no further than today. 'Tis likely she'll be ruined if she remains in London; she had best be sent back to Northumberland.'

'Perhaps we should all go.'

'La, I'm not giving up fun for a bird-witted sister,' Cassie declared. 'Let her go home alone, she deserves it.'

Lady Angel, in spite of her daughters' urging, refused to go to bed. She sat, vinaigrette in hand and hartshorn nearby, and kept up a continuous trickle of complaint of how ill-treated she was and how her nerves were suffering.

'Mama,' Prue interrupted her by saying, 'I have told James, who will tell the other servants, that Selina flew off in a rage to stay with the Courtneys after a quarrel. There is no need to say more. If we are discreet this unhappy affair need not be known.'

'Oh, be sure everyone will know,' her mother lamented, 'and take a fine delight in it! Those stiff-necked girls of Dorcas's will look down their noses and whisper, and I shall be quite undone!'

Prue saw that her mother was determined to dwell upon

the black side of everything, and sent Cassie to order a tray of tea. She was beginning to feel the strain of the past hours, and there was still the confrontation of Selina before them.

Suddenly she heard James crossing the hall and jumping up, she whispered, 'Now Mama, if it is Selina, pray do not go into a tweak over her. She will be in a sad state, and reproaches will overset her further.'

But one glance at her sister's face as she walked into the room told Prue that Selina was suffering neither from shame nor remorse, nor any particular agitation of spirit. She advanced into the room and cast off her pelisse and bonnet, and shook back her fair curls.

'Well, I am glad to see tea and cakes, for I am quite famished. Driving in London is the shabbiest thing, so dirty and noisy. I declare I was shaken to bits before we reached Hammersmith!'

'Selina! Wicked, shameless daughter! You have all but disgraced us and lost your reputation!' Lady Angel wailed furiously.

'Fudge, Mama.' Selina tossed her head, but her colour heightened as she poured herself out a cup of tea. 'You behave like a tragic muse in one of Mr Garrick's plays. I'm back, ain't I?'

'You are a fool, Selina,' Cassie said dispassionately, 'you were near ruined and you know it to be so. You have been saved by the veriest chance.'

'Indeed, I was horrid annoyed with the fuss at the inn! Such a to-do, and when a crowd began to collect I thought it best to leave and come home in a hackney. I was never so mortified in my life, let me tell you.'

Prue, who had been watching her sister, said abruptly, 'I believe you were pleased to be rescued; you had had time to repent your rash behaviour.'

Selina shrugged. 'Perhaps. It was not at all the adventure I had thought. Sir Joseph began to be horrid familiar and after all, I'm not sure I should care to live in France.'

'You shall be returned to Northumberland!' her mother spluttered in high dudgeon. 'You have given us a fine scare, Selina! I'm sure I shall never recover from this night! Such wickedness! Such abandonment of all female propriety! Such cruel lack of feeling for my poor nerves!'

'Laws, Mama, your nerves will recover,' Selina said, helping herself to a slice of cherry cake, 'since I'm back and none the worse. I made a mistake, I grant you. Sir Joseph is not the man I thought him to be; but how is one to know what a man is truly like?'

'By eloping with him, it would seem,' Cassie snapped. 'If you mean to test every beau by running off with him you'll end no better than a Cyprian!'

'Go to your room, Selina,' Prue ordered. 'Come, Mama, Cassie and I shall see you to your bed.' She knew it was best that her mother should not get the chance to gossip with Lizzie in her present emotional state.

There was little sleep for Prue that night. As she tossed uneasily, her mind kept returning to the tall figure of the Duke as he strode to and fro before her. He had saved them from scandal and had, she knew, done it for her. She was deeply grateful, but yet she dreaded meeting him again. This act of his did not wipe out the insult of his offer to make her his mistress. That he was attracted to her, and resented that attraction, was now obvious. Perhaps the resentment would keep him away, and she could learn to forget him.

'I *must* forget him,' she thought. 'I must crush this—this weakness I have. It is shameful that I should think so much of a man who means nothing but my ruin, as surely as Sir Joseph meant my sister's!'

# CHAPTER TWELVE

LADY ANGEL sent for her erring daughter and remained closeted with her for most of the next morning, and Prue's fears were realised when Selina emerged triumphantly with her mother's pardon, and there was no further talk of Northumberland.

'I guessed how it would be,' Cassie said. 'Selina is able to turn Mama's mind as she wishes. I fear Mama's moral principles are somewhat affected since we came to London; she takes her tone from society, and Harry says that despite Their Majesties' primness at court, it is a licentious society, and I agree. Selina will need watching, which will be a great bore.'

On rising, Prue had remembered something the Duke had said, and meeting James in the hall, she asked, 'Did a letter come for me recently, one delivered by hand, I mean?'

'Yes, Miss Prue, the Duke's man delivered it. Did you not get it?'

'I—I may have done, I forget. You did not give it to me direct, I think?'

'No, Miss Prue. Miss Selina said she would take it to you.'

Prue turned away abruptly. So Selina had sought to get even with her! What had the Duke written? She went in search of Selina.

'Why yes, I did take it,' her sister confessed somewhat shamefacedly, 'I wished to pay you out.'

Prue's dark eyes flashed dangerously. 'And read it, I suppose?'

'Oh no, that would have been very wrong! I burned it. I did

not see why you should get notes from the Duke when I was prevented getting anything from Sir Joseph.' She tossed her head and turned away.

Prue decided that only a gallop in the park would cool her indignation and disgust at her sister's behaviour. The groom had just brought her horse around when John Hillier rode up and greeted her with a warmth that did much to raise her spirits. He asked if he might escort her, to which she agreed at once, dismissing her groom.

'Do you attend the rout at Lady Grantly's tonight?' he asked as they entered the park.

'I think not, my mother is taken with the vapours.' She hesitated. 'Does the Duke mean to attend?'

'I do not know. He is in a strange mood, and was out late last night, but not gaming or in society, I think.'

Prue gathered up her reins. 'Come, I shall race you! My horse is impatient for a gallop.'

The air was sweet and fresh and the trees dressed in their full summer glory as they raced. A faint mist lay over the city, giving it a fairylike appearance with spires and cupolas of churches piercing the opal veil. Prue felt her malaise slip from her as the exercise brought quick blood to her cheeks and a sparkle to her dark eyes. John glanced at her appreciatively and murmured,

'London suits you, Mistress Prue, I think.'

Although she told herself she had no wish to see His Grace the Duke again, Prue could not help wondering how he had caused the runaways to be so swiftly intercepted. She also wondered where that faithless husband and seducer of trusting maidens was now, and if he would try to get in touch with her sister again. And of course there was the matter of the letter she had not received. In fact, the more she thought about it, the more she was forced to confess that she *did* wish to meet the Duke, and get answers to these mysteries.

Luckily Lady Angel's foolish tongue could be relied upon

to keep still on the subject of her daughter's behaviour for fear of a scandal. Prue had impressed upon her the necessity for silence, and Selina was not in the way of revealing the unhappy episode.

Prue had just finished a letter to her father when something made her recall the Duke's words: ''Twould be the best thing could you get your sister wed'. She sat, her chin on her hand, her mind busy. Then, turning to her letter, she added another two paragraphs before sealing it with a wafer and calling the footman to take it to the post.

Selina had shown little interest in who had been the instigator of her rescue, and Prue and Cassie persuaded their mother that it was best she should not know but be left to suppose her family had contrived it. Her first defiant attitude had changed, and she appeared out of spirits and lacking her usual vivacity. She accompanied her mother and sisters to parties and routs, but without enthusiasm, and Lady Angel's offer, of tincture of rhubarb and herbal cordials were abruptly refused.

Mrs Courtney had taken a liking to Prue and often included her in a party to attend some entertainment. A visit to Ranelagh was suggested and Prue invited. Hester was greatly pleased to have her friend with her.

'Ranelagh is more exclusive than Vauxhall,' she told Prue as they matched embroidery silks in a shop. 'The concerts in the Rotunda are very fine, and it is possible to walk around the gallery and observe the crowds below. What shall you wear?'

Prue put down a skein of rose silk and considered this important problem.

'The panniered brocade, I think. It is cream, over a gold silk petticoat, with gold lace and rose-red ribbon trimming on neck and sleeve.'

'You will look charming. But everything suits you, Prue. You have looks that can rise above the need for pretty gowns.

It is some enchantment you possess.'

'Faith, that is indeed a pretty compliment,' Prue said, laughing. She turned to the shopman and saw that he was staring past her. She glanced back and saw the Duke of Carlington entering the shop.

'I saw your carriage,' he said, bowing. 'I trust I do not disturb the serious business of choosing silks.'

Prue curtsied demurely. 'We are all but finished, Your Grace, and have supplied ourselves with enough work to keep our fingers busy for six months.'

'And keep them out of mischief, perhaps. I trust your family are in good health?'

She assured him they were. He took her parcels from her and escorted her and her friend to their carriage. As he handed her in, he murmured, 'I shall follow you. I have in mind to call upon Lady Angel.'

'Pray do, Your Grace, she has greatly wished to see you and offer her most grateful thanks.'

'How vastly unfortunate. However, I shall come. I wish to speak to you.'

Hester was interested in the meeting. 'How condescending of him, but I think he admires you, Prue.' She glanced a trifle uneasily at the sudden flush on her friend's charming face. 'He has an unfortunate reputation . . . but of course, men of his distinction are always targets for ill-natured gossip.'

Lady Angel was as emotional and gushingly tearful as Prue had feared. She left the Duke alone with her mother on the pretext of ordering refreshments, in spite of the anguished plea in His Grace's grey eyes as she left the room. If only her mother would behave with more dignity and show greater sensibility!

Harry Dunstan and some friends arrived, and under cover of conversation the Duke drew Prue aside into a window's deep embrasure.

'I do not see your other sister, is she unwell after her

adventure?'

'Oh no, but she is become somewhat subdued and does not care for company now,' Prue explained. 'I pray you will forgive my curiosity, but how did you accomplish her rescue?'

He smiled a trifle grimly and taking out his snuff-box, tapped it before saying, 'Sir Joseph is not discreet in his cups . . . and servants can be bribed. He planned to lie low in the inn at Hammersmith. I believe the lady was not averse from being rescued; she appears to have made no protest.'

'She had realised her mistake,' Prue said quickly. She looked up, meeting his gaze frankly. 'Your Grace, we are indebted to you beyond anything. It is impossible to express our wholehearted gratitude.'

'I want only yours, Prue.' His eyes held hers. 'If you no longer hate me and—what was it? despise me—I shall be satisfied, for the moment.'

She looked away swiftly. 'And where is Sir Joseph now?'

'In France, I suspect. It was . . . made plain to him that his health would benefit by a change of air.'

So Selina was safe, until she lost her head again. Prue's thoughts went to the letter she had written to her father. She came out of her thoughts to hear the Duke ask,

'Shall I see you at Ranelagh on Saturday? Miss Courtney spoke of your joining their party.'

Prue told him she intended to be present, and catching Cassie's eye, begged to be excused.

''Tis Selina,' Cassie hissed in her ear. 'She is in such a way as never was, and I declare I shan't spend time with her!'

'No, not while Harry is here,' Prue replied. 'I shall go to her. Do you prevent Mama from weeping over the Duke.'

Selina was lying on her bed, sobbing miserably.

'I am out of everything! There is no pleasure for me in anything now! I hate London—and I wish I was dead!'

'You don't wish you were at home, do you?'

Selina raised a tear-sodden face. 'I'm sure I couldn't be more unhappy than I am here!'

'Is it about Sir Joseph?'

'No . . . well, yes, I suppose it is. He was so gallant, paid such pretty compliments and said I had won his heart and . . . and now I do not trust *any* man! They are all rakes, and the horridest creatures! And I've made all of you unhappy too!'

Prue sat down beside her and slipped a comforting arm about her shoulders.

'Come, that's a brave admission and shows you in the best light. We are no longer unhappy, but only concerned that you have lost your spirits somewhat. Let us ask Mama to hold a dance here——'

'I should hate it! Smiles and bows and pretty words and protestations of undying passion. . . . All lies! There is not an honest man in London!'

Prue thought it best to say no more. She persuaded her sister to bathe her face with rosewater and put on a pretty gown, and come down to join the company.

She had a moment alone with the Duke before he left and told him his letter had not reached her, but did not say why.

His eyebrows rose. 'Strange. I wished to know if I could be of assistance to your mother in obtaining vouchers for Almack's. My aunt, Lady Anne Bouchier, would sponsor you.'

'Oh, if you *could*!' Prue's eyes sparkled. 'My mother would be highly honoured and pleased.'

'Would *you* be pleased?' His eyes held hers.

'I would indeed appreciate such a favour,' she murmured, and saw his faintly rueful smile as he said,

'I shall set the matter in hand. Pray inform your mother.'

Impulsively she said: 'How wonderfully easy it is for you! You say "my aunt will do this", and with a wave of your hand it will be done!'

'All my wishes are not granted so easily.' There was no

mistaking his meaning. 'But at least you do not hate me, Prue, and perhaps that is not so very far from . . . liking me?'

So he still expected her surrender. She drew back, suddenly chilled, and curtsied before turning away.

Prue knew that she dressed with especial care on Saturday night. Lizzie had to dress her hair twice, and grew impatient at last.

'Lawks, Miss Prue, you're in a fit of the fidgets tonight! The rose wreath is very well.'

'A trifle more forward, I think, Lizzie.'

''Twill ruin it. Anyone would have the notion you were to meet your lover, I declare!'

'Oh, Lizzie, what fudge you talk!' Prue jumped up and shook out the stiff cream brocade that was looped with rose ribbon to show a gold silk petticoat. Little gold slippers, embroidered in gold beads, peeped from beneath the skirt, and her mother's rubies glowed like fire against her creamy skin. 'Give me my fan . . . and scarf—no, not the lace, the Italian gauze, and my perfume flagon . . . the rose perfume, stupid!'

'Stupid, indeed,' the maid grumbled. 'There's no call for you to primp like a country wench at her first ball.'

Prue chuckled as she twirled before the looking-glass.

'Do you mean I am so beautiful I have no need to take trouble?'

Lizzie sniffed as she smoothed a fold in the brocade. 'You'll do, no doubt. But there'll be others as fine, so don't peacock, Miss!'

The first person Prue saw when they entered the gardens was John Hillier, and she knew by the look in his eyes that she was indeed in good looks. Mrs. Courtney liked the young man, and invited him to join her party. Ralph, newly returned from the country, at once engaged him in a discussion about the new cocked hat that had entered the modish world.

''Tis in the military manner, I hear,' he said, 'in white beaver, is it not? One gets confoundedly out of things visiting the country.'

The party occupied one of the boxes around the side of the great Rotunda, and Prue leaned forward to observe the brilliant crowd below. There were plenty of tall men with a faintly arrogant bearing, but the Duke was not one of them. She was uncomfortably aware of a certain dissatisfied sensation at the results of her search. He had said he meant to be present, but no doubt he had changed his mind. Some other entertainment pleased him better . . . or some new beauty had called him to her side!

'May I be allowed to compliment you upon your toilette, Mistress Prue?' John Hillier's words made her turn her head to smile at him. 'You are very lovely tonight—but you are always enchanting, magical!'

'No magic, sir. I am happy, that is all.' She determined not to acknowledge the feeling of disappointment inside her.

''Tis a splendid assembly, is it not? All the world is here.'

'Most of the modish world, certainly. It is rumoured that Their Majesties may appear after attending the play.'

Tea was brought to the box and soon after, a short concert of music held Prue enraptured. John, sitting beside her, kept his eyes on her delicate profile and the sweep of her long dark lashes and tender curve of her lips. When at last she turned, starry-eyed, she was startled at something she saw in his face.

'Mistress Prue,' he burst out in an agitated voice, 'I—I feel I must speak of my feelings. . . . You are for ever in my thoughts, my dreams! You are a flower among women, so lovely——'

'Prue, my dear,' Hester touched her shoulder, 'Mr Harry Dunstan has joined us, and Miss Mandley and Lord Elvery.'

Prue was glad of the interruption. She liked John and valued his friendship, and had begun to hope she had imagined he was falling in love with her, but she was uneasy, remembering the ardent expression on his pleasant young face and the suppressed passion in his voice.

A walk along the upper gallery of the Rotunda was suggested, and the company paired off. Prue found herself with Ralph, to her relief, John being obliged to escort one of the younger Courtney daughters who had been trying to attract his attention all evening.

They were in the gallery when the band struck up the National Anthem, and Prue gazed down with interest to see the Royal party advance into the room and receive the sweeping bow of the Master of Ceremonies before he escorted them to the Royal box. She was not impressed by the Royal presence. She thought the nickname 'Farmer George' suited the red-faced, amiable-looking man, and 'farmer's wife' would not be unsuited to the plump, plain woman beside him!

Suddenly a figure in the royal cortège caught her eye. Surely there could not be two men with so distinguished a bearing, dressed in silver-grey satin? She drew back quickly, aware of a quickening in her blood. It was indeed the Duke, but there was no fear of meeting him; he moved in a circle that she could never enter.

He raised his head, his eyes scanning the circle of boxes lining the room. Was he looking for her? But he would never, never see her in the gallery, and with a mixture of relief and disappointment she continued her promenade with Ralph, who had much to say on the dismal lack of entertainment in the country.

Mrs Courtney greeted her with a smile when she returned to the box.

'We have been honoured by a visit from his Grace the Duke of Carlington. He was unable to remain as His Majesty is tired and does not stay. He enquired for you.' Her smile faded as she motioned Prue to sit beside her. 'Prue, my dear child, is he a close acquaintance? I ask because I have your interest at heart. Even though 'tis possible his reputation is sadly exaggerated, it would be perhaps wise not to—to encourage His Grace.'

Prue lowered her eyes. 'We were able to render a service to the Duke when he met with an accident on the road, and I suppose he feels a trifle of gratitude. That is all, ma'am.'

'I am glad. You have plenty from whom to chose more suitable companions, my dear.'

'Well,' Lizzie demanded that night when she brought Prue her hot milk, 'was the company pleased with you?'

'Oh, la, I was a sensation,' Prue yawned and took her milk. 'The Queen curtsied to me and the King blew me a kiss, and ten young blades declared their passion for me. 'Twas a fine an evening as I'd expected.'

But she knew the evening had not been quite so fine as she had expected . . . or hoped.

# CHAPTER THIRTEEN

PRUE was sitting at her embroidery one morning when she was startled to hear her mother say thoughtfully,

'I have decided that a trip to the coast would benefit us all. Sea air is declared excellent for one's health by doctors and my nerves have been quite worn down by recent events. Dorcas has gone to Weymouth, in Dorset. She insists it is for Caro's chest, but I am not taken in. The young Lord Felton, just come into his title and fortune, is in Weymouth, and Dorcas has a great notion of him for Caro. She says it is easy to find comfortable lodgings. What think you of my plan, Prue my dear?'

Prue looked up eagerly from her work, her eyes sparkling.

'It is a famous notion, Mama! I should like it above all things! London grows so hot and dirty, and such a change may rouse Selina's spirits, perhaps, she has been sadly mopish of late. When shall we go?'

'I shall arrange the matter at once; Dorcas has given me addresses.'

Prue was enchanted, and Selina showed some unusual animation when told of the idea. Cassie thought the plan agreeable, her only sorrow being separation from Harry.

Lodgings were engaged, and the London house left in the care of the staff. Only William, the footman, and Lizzie accompanied the family on their expedition to Weymouth.

The sun was blazing down on the city the day they left it. The streets had a rank smell and the air a staleness. Street hawkers, milk-sellers, pie vendors, fresh-water sellers and ballad singers bawling unmusically made Prue rejoice that she was leaving London as Lawson, with William up beside him, drove the chaise through the noisy cluttered streets and, at last, into the freshness of open fields and pretty woodlands. She sighed contentedly and lay back among her cushions.

''Twas an inspiration, Mama, to leave the city for Dorset. What caused you to think of it? I suppose it was Mrs Beauford, was it not?'

'What, child? Oh yes, that was how it came about,' Lady Angel said in abstracted tones. She was gazing out of the window, her expression unusually complacent.

The inn they put up in was reasonably clean, and the landlord obliging. Lizzie had brought sheets, not trusting what might be provided. Next morning they set off and made good time with rested horses and a dry and not ill-kept road.

As they drew near the coast, it seemed to Prue that the air took on a sparkle and an invigorating salty tang. It was late afternoon when they reached the small, bow-fronted house facing the sea and met their landlady, a respectable widow who let apartments to the gentry. Even Lady Angel found nothing to grumble at in the rooms and meal served them. That night Prue went to sleep lulled by the gentle surge and retreat of waves upon the beach.

Next morning Lady Angel was weary from the journey and Selina declared her head ached from the jolting in the chaise, but Prue and Cassie were up betimes and after breakfast, set out to walk along the front and admire the deep blue of the sea now flecked with small fishing-boats, and watch the children playing on the strand with their nurses while their parents strolled to and fro, greeting acquaintances. The little town had become popular with the world of fashion since Royalty had patronised it, and the presence of handsome bucks and their ladies gave it an air of elegance that increased its natural charm.

Cassie pinched Prue's arm suddenly and said: 'There are

the Beaufords! Let us turn and pretend we do not see them! 'Tis a pity they should be here, the girls bore me excessively.'

'Alas, we cannot,' Prue sighed, 'they have already observed us.'

'So you are come at last,' Mrs Beauford remarked. 'I trust the journey did not prove too tiring for your worthy mother. But, my dear creatures, I must suggest you wear veils! The sea air is positively cruel to the female complexion.'

'There is an establishment in the town where you can buy such veils,' Caro said, 'and they are not expensive.'

Mrs Beauford asked if Lady Angel was receiving visitors, and on being told by Prue that her mother had probably risen by now, decided to accompany the two girls back to their lodgings.

'You are come at an excellent time, Clarissa,' Mrs Beauford remarked on meeting her friend, 'I declare half London is here. There will be no lack of genteel society. I suppose you will be visiting Abbotstone? 'Tis but a few miles from here.'

Something in her voice made Prue glance at her and say: 'Abbotstone, ma'am?'

'Why for sure! Do not pretend to me you are unaware that the Duke of Carlington's great estate lies near the town!'

Prue turned swiftly and caught her mother's gratified smile.

'Yes indeed, my dear Dorcas. His Grace has honoured us with an invitation which I have accepted, an invitation to drive over to Abbotstone and take refreshment with him tomorrow.'

'I'm sure I rejoice to hear it,' her friend said acidly. 'For myself, I should not care to subject my daughters to . . . But no doubt you know your own business best.'

'Oh yes, I do,' Lady Angel agreed. 'And now tell me what entertainment the town offers.'

Prue sat letting the conversation wash over her. So her

mother had known the Duke's estate was in the neighbourhood of Weymouth when she decided to visit the town! It was even possible that it had been the reason for leaving London! Prue felt her cheeks burn at the thought of her mother's lack of all proper feeling. To have pursued him so openly and taken advantage of his recent assistance in the matter of Selina's elopement! To solicit an invitation—she was fairly certain that it *had* been solicited—from a man so much above them. It was not to be tolerated! She would refuse to go to Abbotstone.

But Lady Angel would brook no opposition.

'You shall not disgrace us all, Prue, with your missish ways! If it had not been for His Grace your sister would be ruined by now.'

'That does not give us the right to thrust ourselves upon him,' Prue protested sharply. 'I have no wish to meet him.'

'I insist you shall!' Her mother's plump face had become an angry red. 'You are more a fool than I thought you, daughter! You need some plain speaking. Fanny's money will not last for ever. You and your sisters are come to London to make suitable marriages, and so you shall! Selina nearly ruined herself, but she has seen her error and will soon find a husband among the young blades who flutter around her. Cassie can give up all notion of Harry, I have other plans for her. She does not, thank heaven, have your undutiful nature! You, Prue, have the best chance. This friendship with His Grace, if you use your head, can lead to great things for all of us!'

Prue sprang up, her dark eyes afire. ''Tis I who shall now speak plainly! The Duke will never have a thought of marrying me, *never*—and it is *you* who are foolish to imagine such a thing! The Duke does not marry—he takes a mistress when a woman attracts his notice! And you will be thought a vastly complaisant mother if you foster this acquaintance with him! Why, you would be considered little better than Mother

Banks of Curzon Street!'

'*Prue*!' Lady Angel shrieked. 'Oh, wicked wretch! How dare you speak so to me! I have brought you to London——'

'To sell me to the highest bidder?' Prue demanded fiercely. 'Would you wish me to attach the Duke by such means? *Would* you?'

'No, of course not! I am persuaded he would never attempt such behaviour,' Lady Angel protested. 'I mean only that he is of the highest importance in the fashionable world and could be vastly useful. . . . Why, you said yourself that he will procure us tickets for Almack's. And there is no knowing what else might come of his patronage.'

Prue turned abruptly, her anger turning to a sick realisation of how easily her mother had taken to the cynicism of the grand society. Ambition, vanity, greed, surely these were new in her? Or had they lain dormant, awaiting favourable conditions?

There was no help for it, Lady Angel made it plain that she would take all her daughters to Abbotstone.

Lizzie helped Prue dress next morning.

'The worked muslin, Miss Prue, with primrose ribbon knots,' she decreed, 'and the Italian scarf, 'tis too warm for a pelisse, and the wired lace cap.'

'No, I'll have a straw to shade my face,' Prue said, 'and my hair dressed in country style. We are not in London now, Lizzie.'

'But His Grace the Duke——'

'Must be content with my straw hat,' Prue announced firmly, snatching up a wide Leghorn trimmed with primrose ribbon and going down to join her sisters at the door.

Deliberately she kept her thoughts off the man she was to meet. That her mother had discovered he was to be in residence in Dorset for a time she was now certain, and had managed to let him know that she planned to visit Weymouth. What must he think of them? What would he think of *her* agreeing to this barefaced pursuit?

'The sea air gives you a fine colour, Prue,' Cassie remarked as they drove off, 'and Selina looks less like a plucked chicken. How I should enjoy it all, if only. . . .' She fell silent, her eyes dreamy.

They drove inland, the country spreading out around them in fair fields and woods and small farms. A fresh sea breeze kept the heat of the day at bay as they drove through narrow lanes bordered with flowery hedgerows. Mob-capped women bobbed curtsies and farm labourers touched caps, and soon they came to a great stone gatehouse flanked with octagonal towers. The gates were swung open for them and they entered a long stretch of parkland holding handsome stands of oak and beech, copses of larch and birch, and a flash of water where a lake lay reflecting the brilliance of the sky.

'Indeed, a most splendid property!' Lady Angel exclaimed, her eyes bright as she stared around her. 'I believe the house is even finer. Here comes a horseman . . . why, 'tis the Duke himself!'

He came riding up on a splendid sorrel mare. His bare head was unpowdered, and sunlight caught the bronze lights in his thick hair.

It was the first time Prue had seen him in country clothes; somehow he looked larger and more formidable. After a few words of welcome, he accompanied them up to the house and she saw how well he managed his horse and, despite his informal attire, how distinguished he looked.

John Hillier's account had prepared her for the magnificence of the ducal house, but not for its beauty. Sunlight warmed the red brick frontage and set fire to the many mullioned windows. Gables and turrets rose up against the high blue sky, and the front entrance—a semi-circular arch flanked by classical columns—was surmounted by a carved stone shield holding the arms of the family.

Lady Angel was led into the huge hall, exclaiming

ecstatically at all she saw. Prue, looking at the carved oak staircase that went up at right-angles to a gallery, the panelled walls hung with tapestries, mediaeval shields and swords and heavy oil paintings, caught her breath at such noble grandeur.

The room the Duke led them into looked on to an Italian garden where white marble fauns and nymphs gleamed against dark yews, and a sunken pool held pearly water-lilies. Prue was unable to restrain a little cry of pleasure.

'Oh, 'tis the prettiest thing!'

'A charming conceit,' His Grace said, turning to her. 'My mother had gardeners brought from Florence to make it. Beyond is a fine rose garden that I believe worth seeing.'

Three footmen in splendid livery now brought in wine, negus and lemonade, cold meats, fruit and a bewildering variety of small cakes.

'Such elegant luxury,' Lady Angel sighed, accepting a glass of Malaga.

The girls chose lemonade, in which sliced strawberries floated. After a few minutes had passed, John Hillier came in and bowed to the visitors.

'Where is the company?' the Duke asked him.

'The ladies are picking strawberries, your Grace, 'tis their latest whim, though I've told them the fruit may stain their finery,' John told him, 'and the gentlemen are not yet returned from riding in the park.'

'When they return, tell them I await them in the Italian salon.'

Prue was looking around her at the charming room whose walls were hung with pale green silk. Curtains of gold silk draped the long windows and Italian-type furniture on white carpets gave the room a delicacy she found delightful.

'Do you care for pretty china, Mistress Prue?' the Duke asked. 'There is a somewhat fine collection in the——'

He was interrupted by the entry of his guests, and had to turn to greet and introduce them. The ladies, like colourful butterflies, swept curtsies and shot assessing glances at the newcomers, and the gentlemen made graceful legs as they bowed and looked with approval at the twins' golden beauty and at Prue, bewitching in her dainty muslin and primrose ribbons.

Everywhere Prue looked she saw luxury, richness, beauty. Treasures brought from far countries, elegant furniture fashioned by masters of their art, and banks of hothouse blooms. Luxury such as this could be hers if she so chose—but not by honourable means! If she became the Duke's mistress she would have all a woman could desire—except a wedding ring. His home, his London house, the palace in Florence, castle in Scotland, his wealth and protection would be hers . . . and his love.

Her heart began to beat in heavy, uneven strokes. The luxury, wealth and worldly possessions, these could never entice her. But to know the love of the man whose kisses had made her a woman, kisses that haunted her still; to see his grey eyes become passionate, tender, loving; to feel his arms around her, holding her against his heart. . . .

She turned and walked blindly to the window and leant her hot forehead against the cool pane. This was madness! This was terrible danger! This—oh, surely this could not be . . . love? Her heart could not betray her in so cruel a manner. To feel love for a man who planned her ruin! She must bury such love, bury it deep, and forget it.

'I have yet to show you my collection of German and Italian porcelain.' The Duke's voice behind her sent a shiver through her. 'If you will allow me.' He held out his arm and, trembling, she laid the tips of her fingers on it and went with him out of the room, across the hall to a smaller room lined with books and where there was a magnificent cabinet displaying a priceless collection of porcelain.

As the footman shut the door behind them, the Duke turned to face her, a smile softening the sternness of his eyes.

'I bid you welcome to my home, Prue. What do you think of it?'

'It is . . . very magnificent, Your Grace. I am not used to such a display of elegance. I wish to say something.' She raised her chin, schooling herself to meet his eyes coolly. 'I did not know, when my mother suggested coming to Weymouth, that your estate lay so near. And I did *not* know she had solicited an invitation, or that invitation would have been refused.'

He raised his brows. 'Now, why should you refuse me the delight of your company? It is my pleasure to offer you and your family hospitality.'

'I think it best we do not indulge you in that pleasure. I must request you not to invite us again, and to forget we are in Dorset.'

'You ask the impossible, you enchanting creature!' He caught her hands, pulling her to him. 'Prue, I will not let you escape me. You are disturbing my peace of mind rather too disastrously! I could make you happy; we could find enchantment together. You have not known love, yet you are made for it! Stop playing with me, Prue,' his voice roughened as his hands tightened on hers, 'I mean to have you! We can live abroad, if you so wish, or——'

She dragged her hands away, a sudden surge of courage and anger sweeping her into passionate protest.

'Indeed, sir, 'tis time I spoke plainly! You offer me disgrace! You think to lure me with promises of luxury and wealth. I will have none of it—or of you! You are mistaken if you think I must fall easy victim to your plans. You have once given me cause to feel gratitude, and that gratitude is all I shall ever feel for you. Even if it were—were possible I had a tenderness for you, I would never, never accept your terms! Speak no more of this to me!'

He was silent and she saw his mouth tighten into a thin line and his eyes narrow, and for a second she was afraid.

He said softly: 'You shall be mine yet, Prue, I do not accept defeat. You are angry because you must struggle against your wish to surrender.'

'Oh, 'tis false! A wicked lie!' She swung around to see the door open and a slim, pretty woman peer in.

'*Ma foi*, Charles, your guests think it strange you disappear like . . .' she fluttered a slim hand, '. . . a puff of wind.' She came into the room, looking with frank interest at Prue's blazing eyes and warm cheeks. 'Is Charles being naughty, ma'am? Oh la! He is not to be trusted.' She had an attractive trace of foreign accent. 'You are too pretty to hide from the gentlemen for so long. Come, we lead naughty Charles back to the salon, yes?'

'Elise,' the Duke sounded incensed, 'I will not allow you to——'

'La, I think you will have to, sweet cousin.' She turned to Prue. 'He is my cousin and *such* a bad one, alas! Let us leave him, *mademoiselle*, to frown and make faces!'

She caught Prue's hand and pulled her out of the room. Outside, she glanced shrewdly at Prue and murmured, 'Charles tries to make love and you do not wish it I think.'

Prue stiffened, then suddenly she smiled. It was not possible to take offence with such a pretty, butterfly little creature.

'Is it his habit to make love to his women guests?'

'Perhaps not,' she put her head on one side, her bright birdlike eyes running over Prue,' but you are *très charmante*. Let us become friends. I find you are not a mouse as so many English ladies are. You make Charles angry, and it is good for him.'

Her name, Prue discovered, was Elise de la Fournes, and she was staying at the house with her mother, a formidable lady in maroon satin. A couple of gallants eagerly offered to show Prue and her new friend around the rose garden, and Prue was glad of the opportunity to recover her composure.

When she returned to the house, Lady Angel was, somewhat reluctantly, asking for her carriage to be brought around.

'I shall call upon you soon, Mademoiselle Angel,' Elise whispered to Prue, 'now that I see you are not so *very* angelic! Charles sometimes calls me *petite diable*, so we shall be friends.'

As they drove away Cassie remarked: 'What a strange creature that French girl was; she says the strangest things.'

'An impertinent little miss,' Lady Angel snapped. 'Do not encourage her, Prue.'

'I like her,' Prue said quietly, 'and I shall welcome her as a friend.'

'Prue! I will not tolerate such open defiance! You are sadly changed!'

'I believe we are all changed, ma'am.' Prue met her mother's angry eyes and saw them falter and drop. 'Perhaps it were better had we never received poor Aunt Fanny's inheritance.'

She turned resolutely away, shutting her ears to her mother's shrill protests. It would have been better, far better, she was thinking, if they had never picked up a wounded gentleman from a ditch and she had never met the mocking grey eyes of His Grace the Duke of Carlington.

# CHAPTER FOURTEEN

LADY ANGEL resisted all pleading to return to London, hoping, Prue suspected, for another invitation to Abbotstone. But Prue was determined to avoid the Duke at all costs now that she was aware of a dismaying weakness towards him, and Cassie had begun to pine for Harry, and even Selina was showing signs of becoming restless and declared the dashing bucks she met were all of a likeness, and vastly boring.

Clouds appeared on the horizon, threatening rain and an end to the fine weather. Selina, drumming her fingers on the window pane, turned to Prue. 'Let us go walking before the rain comes and keeps us within. Cassie is busy writing a letter.'

Prue agreed, and they set out to walk along the sea-front, finding the quick, cool wind exhilarating and their skirts somewhat unmanageable.

'Have you news from Papa?' Selina asked, clutching at her billowing muslin.

'I had a letter forwarded from London. He seems well.'

'*I* had a letter from Northumberland this morning.'

'So I observed.'

'I am glad you did not remark upon it, since Mama did not observe it, luckily.' Selina made for a sheltered seat and sank down on to it. ''Twas from Jim West. He asks for an answer,' she said carelessly. 'I think I may give it.'

'Is all well with him?'

'Oh yes, very well indeed.' She turned to Prue, her careless air gone and her face bright. 'His old uncle has died, and Jim receives his fortune and plans to buy Beechwood Manor and set up for himself. Is it not prime news?'

'Beechwood is a pretty house and the land is well set out,' Prue agreed. 'Jim will make a good thing of it.' She glanced at her sister. 'He will be quite a catch now, will he not? I've no doubt the Misses Smith will be setting their caps at him!'

Selina sat up. 'Those sallow creatures? Jim would not look at them!'

'Why not, since *you* refuse to look at him? Jim is a good fellow with a most honest heart. Oh, he will be caught before long, you may count on it.'

Selina was silent, her eyes on the sea now fretted into surging waves by the wind. A fine mist of sea-spray invaded their shelter, and the girls rose and hastened back to their lodgings. A smart little phaeton stood before the door and Selina cried, 'La, I believe it is your little French friend!'

Elise fluttered to meet them when they entered the sitting-room. '*Voilà*! You see I have come! Mama suffers from the migraine and requires much attention.' She screwed up her face quaintly. 'Faugh! I do not make a good nurse!'

Prue laughed and sat down to chat with her new friend. Elise amused her with her bubbling spirits, outspoken comments and lightly cynical view of life. If there was no great depth of character, there was a sparkle and a gaiety that appealed to Prue, but when Elise announced her intention of bringing her friend back to Abbotstone, Prue began hastily to find excuses.

Elise smiled knowingly. 'Charles is away, *mon amie*. He takes the company to Dorchester for the day. And see, the rain has blown over. You shall come. You will not be nervous because I drive you? I am very good, you know. Charles lets me take the phaeton out alone.'

Prue glanced at her. 'Are you *perfectly* sure he does?'

'Perhaps not,' Elise said with engaging candour, 'but today he is not here. You will come?'

It was too tempting to refuse. To get away from her mother's ill-temper and Cassie's sighs and, most of all, her own restlessness of spirit. *He* would not be there, so she would be safe and could explore the grounds with a charming companion.

Lady Angel was all complaisance, and Prue did not think it necessary to mention the Duke's absence. They set off and she soon saw that Elise was indeed an excellent driver and handled the reins with admirable assurance.

The swift passage of rain-clouds had driven off the oppressive heat and put a sparkle on the countryside, and Prue drew in a breath of the sweet-scented air and cried, 'How delightful it must be to live here all the year!'

Elise flicked the horse lightly with the whip. 'Oh, I should find it vastly boring! One would become a vegetable.'

Prue laughed. It was indeed difficult to imagine her friend being satisfied for long with the beauties of sea and a land where gently rolling hills and little villages lay hidden.

A groom took the carriage away and Elise ran up the steps of the porch crying,

'I shall show you my new *robe à l'anglaise*, it is very beautiful and I shall be a sensation when I go to London.'

She led the way to her room, a charming apartment in the Chinese style. The gold-and-black lacquered bed had green silk curtains, and embroidered silk panels hung from tasselled rods on the walls.

After admiring Elise's gown, and the jewels and Spanish lace fan, Prue begged to see the rose garden, and together they wandered the grassy paths amid cream, rose, yellow, pink and crimson blooms that filled the air with delicious perfume. Prue was standing under a pergola, a few crimson petals fallen on her glossy curls, laughing at Elise who had raced after a butterfly, when some instinct made her turn her head, and she saw the Duke standing a few yards behind her, watching her with smiling grey eyes. He was in riding clothes of the plain colours and material suitable for country wear, but the immaculate cut was of a London tailor.

She caught her breath. 'Your Grace. . . . We did not expect you!'

'*Tiens!* You are supposed to be riding to Dorchester, Charles,' Elise cried, turning. 'We do not wish you here! Why do you return, please?'

He came towards them with lazy strides, swinging his riding crop.

'I fear your mother's migraine returned and she decided to come back so, naturally, I escorted her.' He bowed slightly and Prue knew he was amused at their consternation.

Elise tossed her head. 'Phoo! It is my belief you persuaded her because you guessed I intended to invite Mistress Prue Angel to visit me! Someone speaks of it. . . .' Her eyes narrowed. 'Ah! The groom! I tell him I wish the phaeton today! He is wicked! I tell him he is not to speak of it!'

'He's quite right to tell me. You are not supposed to drive alone, my dear cousin. Yes, I suspected you wished to visit Mistress Prue and, as you have often expressed excessive boredom with Weymouth, that you would invite her to Abbotstone.' He brushed a cream rose-leaf from his sleeve and turned to Prue. 'What think you of my roses?'

She had recovered from her moment of shock and was able to say calmly that the garden well deserved its reputation. Now he was here, she would have to make the best of it, but if he attempted to get her alone, she would insist on being sent back to Weymouth.

Slightly to her surprise, he made no such attempt, and when at last Elise reluctantly decided that she should see how her mother did, he escorted Prue to the library and left her there.

Elise reappeared, saying gaily that her mother suffered

nothing more than her usual vapours on being required to move from her armchair in the salon and go driving, and suggested she show Prue some of the famous rooms of the mansion. The Duke soon joined them, and Prue began to enjoy herself in a way she had not thought possible. The Duke's account of the history of the great house, and stories of his ancestors whose portraits hung in the long, panelled picture gallery, interested her deeply. His manner was that of a genial, thoughtful host, his attentions such as a man of breeding would accord a welcome guest under his roof. He teased Elise until she broke into a torrent of scolding French, and assured her she would set all London by the ears when her mother took her there.

'You go soon to the city?' Prue asked her friend.

'Oh yes, very soon I hope. I am much excited! It will be charming to flirt with the—as you say it—dashing blades!' She broke into laughter, her dark eyes sparkling mischievously.

Refreshments were brought and served on the long stone terrace under the blind gaze of marble cupids toying with their bows. The sun had broken through the clouds and lay, a pale golden patina, over the gardens and long vistas of lawn and wood.

'Does John go with the company today?' Elise asked suddenly.

'No, he has business to do for me in Weymouth,' the Duke told her, tilting back in his chair, his eyes on a flight of white doves.

'Weymouth? I did not meet him.'

'I am excessively glad you did not, dear cousin, or you would have most certainly seen to it that he did no business today.'

Elise pouted. 'You make him work too much, Charles.'

'He has to earn his salary, which he does very satisfactorily.'

'He goes with you when you return to London?'

'Of course.' His eyebrows rose a trifle. 'You do not expect me to manage my life without him?'

'Oh, la! You are lazy, Charles!' She turned to Prue. 'He does nothing, but *nothing*, except what he wishes to do!'

He laughed suddenly and Prue turned in some surprise and met his eyes. His face had lost the stern lines and had a charm that caught at her heart, sending a quiver through her. How lucky he laughed somewhat seldom, or she might be undone! She knew she was enjoying her day, and was happy and filled with a tremulous excitement which she must conceal. She also knew she was deliberately ignoring her heart's warning that she was playing with fire, that the power he had over her was steadily increasing and could overwhelm her if she did not strengthen her defences.

When he handed her into the chaise and did not suggest he accompany her back to Weymouth, she was torn between chagrin and relief. On the drive back she had much to think of and make her uneasy. That she was falling in love with a man who would never marry her seemed to her all too likely. She was deeply aware of him when he was with her, of his lean strength, his naturally arrogant bearing, the occasional harshness in his face and his grey eyes that could blaze with a light that made her weak, or turn to chill steel. He wanted her; it was possible he had love for her, but such love she could never accept. His terms shamed her!

Suddenly she found burning tears filling her eyes. She must leave Dorset, and at once! She must persuade her mother, somehow.

Fortune favoured her. As she came up the stairs of their lodgings, she met Lizzie with her arms full of clothes.

'What goes on, Lizzie?' she asked in surprise.

The maid sniffed and tossed her head. 'Her ladyship has it in her head that we must all return to London tomorrow! And

I have but this afternoon washed her yellow silk stockings and linen shift!'

Cassie was outside the sitting-room door. She caught Prue's arm and whispered, 'Oh, sister, such a set-up as never was! Caro Beauford has caught young Lord Felton and the engagement will be in the *Morning Post*, and Mama is in such a way as you cannot guess!'

Lady Angel was indeed in a sad state. 'Dorcas has called solely to crow it over me now that her daughter is to marry a lord!' she burst out on seeing Prue. 'And I was forced to listen to her peacocking and give my good wishes! I was never so humiliated! I, with three handsome daughters who have attached no one, and that ginger puss of Dorcas's with a man who has both title and wealth! 'Tis not to be borne! I am sadly disappointed in you, daughters! I have put myself to great trouble for you, and see how you repay me!'

'Indeed, Mama, I feel for you,' Prue said soothingly. 'We came to find husbands and here we are, three spinsters still. Is this why we return to London?'

'I shall not stay to have Dorcas parading Lord Felton before my eyes every minute,' Lady Angel snapped. 'I want no more of her; she has ever been a false friend and of little use to us. Lizzie is to pack today, do you go and help her. I am done with Weymouth!'

The twins left the room, Cassie looking radiant. As Prue turned to follow them, her mother said,

'Stay, was the Duke at Abbotstone today?'

'He had started out with his guests to visit Dorchester.' It was not necessary, Prue considered, to add that he had seen fit to return.

'So, as yet we can expect no more there.' Lady Angel pursed her mouth, considering. 'However, we shall have Almack's Assembly when we return. Lady Anne Bouchier has requested we call so that you girls can be presented to her, and then she will obtain vouchers for us. You will meet most elegant company there, and perhaps . . .'

Prue escaped before her mother had elucidated her hopes. Her wish had been granted and they were to return to London, where it would be easier to avoid the Duke, should he still wish to pursue her. His change of manner *could* mean that he had lost interest in her. No doubt easier conquests were to hand. And it was possible that her attraction for him had simply been her refusal to accept his terms, and to fall victim to his noble standing in the world and his wealth and power. He was used to easy conquests and her rejection had intrigued him . . . but only for a short while.

'He will soon forget me,' she thought as she went to her room, 'and I shall forget him—or I shall find no happiness in life!'

# CHAPTER FIFTEEN

ONCE back in London, preparations for the evening at Almack's Assembly Rooms claimed Lady Angel's attention, and her mortification at Caro's triumph was in some degree eased on learning that Mrs Beauford had *not* succeeded in getting vouchers for that most exclusive club. There was the important visit to Lady Anne Bouchier to present the Angel girls, and the serious business of gowns for the occasion. Luckily she was so engrossed in all this that she failed to note a certain lack of enthusiasm in her daughters.

'Oh, I expect I may enjoy something in it,' Cassie said as the sisters sat together in the morning-room. ''Twill be a triumph for us to appear, and no doubt the company will be very fine, but Harry will not be there.'

'And that will spoil the evening for you, I suppose.' Prue looked at her sister with troubled eyes. 'Cassie, I do not wish to be unkind or to interfere, but you must be aware that Mama is quite set against poor Harry.'

'Oh, so she tells me frequently! She has a noble young sprig in mind for me, although he is a swaggerer and vastly boring.' There was an unusual look of determination on Cassie's face. 'I am not Caro Beauford, to be pushed into a loveless marriage because my mother wishes it. You had best know that Harry has said he loves me, and he knows I love him. He was taken with Prue at first,' she added frankly, 'and thought me too forward. But I have won his heart, and he will journey to Northumberland in the autumn to speak to Papa.'

'You will put Mama in a sad way,' Selina remarked. She

was sitting by the window looking dreamily out at the busy street. '*I* do not plan to marry at all. 'Tis for you, Prue, to put Dorcas Beauford in her place by making some splendid match.' She leaned forward suddenly. 'The Courtney coach is at the door.'

Mrs Courtney and her daughters had come to pay a call upon the Angel family and enquire how they enjoyed their visit to Dorset. Prue was delighted to see Hester, and soon the two girls had seated themselves in a corner and were deep in interesting conversation.

'Oh, there has been a fine scandal about a German prince and one of the ladies of the town they call Dally the Tall, and he has been recalled to the German court, no less,' Hester told her. 'And 'tis rumoured that two titled gentlemen have been ruined gaming at White's and have fled the city.'

'I fear I have brought you nothing of great concern from Weymouth,' Prue said. 'If there was scandal, I did not hear it.'

'But you must tell me of your visit there.'

Prue told her, among other things, of her visits to Abbotstone, and saw her friend's quick glance.

'My mother saw to it that the Duke was aware we came to Dorset,' she said wryly, 'it was not of my seeking. However, he was a pleasant host, and I have made a charming little friend of his cousin,' and she told Hester about Elise.

They discussed the visit to Almack's and Prue chuckled as she told how Lady Anne, a redoubtable old lady, had agreed, on inspection, to take them under her wing, and had put them in the way of how they must behave on their first appearance.

'I shall be vastly nervous, Hester.'

'You will be a vast success, my dear Prue,' Hester said, smiling, 'It will be yet another triumph for you.'

John Hillier called to beg the honour of escorting them to Almack's, as he too was to attend the assembly. Prue was pleased to see him although she feared it meant the Duke was in London.

'My lord Duke remains in Dorset,' John said, calming her fears. 'His guests are gone, except for Madame de la Fournes and her daughter.'

'Is Mademoiselle Elise content to remain at Abbotstone now the company has gone?' Prue asked.

John smiled. 'I think not. She begs her mother to take her to London. She is not in love with country life.'

'I hope she comes,' Prue exclaimed, 'I value her friendship.'

John hesitated, as if about to say something, but when he next spoke it was to suggest she should ride with him in the park next morning, to which she gladly consented.

The twins had chosen white embossed satin for their new gowns, and their heads dressed in the new towering edifice of feathers, flowers and ribbon built upon a frame. Lady Angel, too, prepared to dazzle the assembly with a display of magnificent if top-heavy example of the coiffeur's art, and Prue was criticised for her insistence on a simple arrangement of primroses and leaf-green velvet ribbon to dress her dark hair.

Her gown was primrose brocade and made in the shorter version of the polonaise, which revealed her pretty ankles and dainty silver kid shoes with oblong buckles backed with green ribbon. The skirt was looped back to show a flowered silk petticoat, and a tiny frivolous apron of lace completed the charming toilette. Necklet and earrings of aquamarines were her only jewels, and the Duke's fan hung from her wrist as she followed her mother into the coach on the night of the assembly.

As they joined the throng of carriages making for King Street, Prue felt that perhaps she was going to enjoy the evening more than she expected. At least there would be dancing, and John Hillier would be there, faithfully attentive, to bolster her self-confidence. The twins had become somewhat silent, awed by what lay before them.

Lady Angel, surveying her flock, smiled in high satisfaction. They were all three beauties and would attract attention and, she hoped, husbands!

She was correct in thinking that her daughters would be noticed. Partners appeared with flattering regularity and even Selina, who had not been in good spirits for some days, brightened enough to flirt with her circle of beaux. Obeying their sponsor's dictum, the girls behaved with circumspection and had the gratification of seeing that lady smile upon them, and hearing her confide to a friend that they were a pretty trio of beauties with refined manners.

'Positive angels, 'pon honour!' a dandified buck exclaimed as he led Cassie out to dance. ''Tis not often we are blessed with heavenly visitation!'

Prue was standing up with John in a country dance when she chanced to glance at the door and saw, to her amazement, Elise de la Fournes standing looped, be-ribboned, jewelled and powdered until she was a veritable butterfly indeed. Behind her loomed the mountainous figure of her mother, Madame de la Fournes.

Prue felt a surge of pleasure on seeing her pretty friend and turned, smiling, to look up at John and say, 'Do you observe that Mademoiselle Elise has come? Is that not delightful?'

John was looking at her, his eyes intent on her glowing face and great soft, dark eyes now alight with pleasure, and he did not appear to hear her. When she repeated her remark, he said, without taking his eyes off her,

'I believe she had hopes of attending the assembly.'

'I am *so* glad to see her.' Prue turned to look at her friend again and received a shock. Elise was staring at her with angry eyes, and her small face was curiously tight. She turned away abruptly and Prue, suddenly chilled, felt she must have imagined what she had seen. Why should Elise be angry with her? Elise must have seen something elsewhere that had annoyed her, that must be the explanation.

When, some time later, Elise ran up to exclaim at meeting her, her smile was as enchanting as ever and Prue knew she must have mistaken the odd expression that she had surprised on her friend's pretty face. Elise explained she had insisted on her mother bringing her to London as she was *bien ennuyée de* Dorset.

'Did I not see John with you?' she asked, looking around her. 'I suppose you met him here.'

'He very kindly escorted us here,' Prue told her.

'Ah, John has always a kind heart,' Elise said lightly. 'He takes pity on people who are not perfectly *au fait* with society.'

'You mean us?' Prue asked, smiling.

'Oh no. . . . Ah! There he is!' Her small face lit up and she waved her fan at John, who was crossing the room. 'Now I shall dance with him. John is a very fine dancer.'

Left alone, Prue watched John lead Elise out to dance. An uncomfortable idea was taking shape in her mind. Elise's expression on seeing John had not escaped her. Did the pretty butterfly have a *tendresse* for the Duke's secretary? Probably she had flirted with him at Abbotstone, more for something to relieve boredom than for any deeper reason. She was laughing up into John's face, saying something that by his averted face did not greatly please him.

The knowledge that she was admired and sought by partners was a heady experience, and Prue's spirits rose as she flirted her fan and acknowledged compliments, and saw the occasional sour look thrown at her by wallflowers and their even sourer mothers. The twins, too, were enjoying their triumph and Lady Angel, very upright under her towering head-dress, smiled graciously on handsome young blades attired gorgeously in satins and velvets when they returned her daughters to her after the dance.

At last the evening came to an end and Prue sought Elise.

'Do you stay at Cavendish Square?' She hesitated a moment, then went on with an effort: 'Does the Duke come to London also?'

'*Ma foi!* I do not know. Charles pleases himself. Perhaps he may come. Prue,' she caught Prue's hand, 'poor Mama is feeling unwell and I shall ask John to escort us home. You do not mind?'

'Oh no, not at all. Here he comes.' Prue, slightly disconcerted, moved away but not before she had seen the look of vexation on John's face as Elise began to address him and hoped sincerely that Elise had not seen it also.

In the coach, when she explained John's absence, Cassie said, 'Well, your friend was shamming. I heard Madame remarking that she was in fine health after Dorset, there was nothing vapourish about her.'

'She wanted to take John away from Prue,' Selina said knowingly. 'It was plain he did not wish to attend her, but she would have it.'

Prue was silent, feeling unhappy and disturbed. If Elise saw her as a rival it could be the end of their friendship.

''Twas the greatest pity the dear Duke could not attend tonight,' Lady Angel said, breaking into Prue's uneasy thoughts, 'but he comes to town soon, Madame de la Fournes tells me. No doubt we shall have the honour of meeting him again.'

Prue's heart lurched, and for a second her breath failed her. A wave of emotion, so strong that she had to turn away lest her face betray her, swept through her. Fear and dismay battled with a longing that pierced her like a sword. To see him again, to have to dissemble, to fight this treacherous weakness. . . . Was she strong enough? How cruel that her heart should betray her with a man she should, she *must*, force herself to forget. Why could she have not loved John, who loved her honourably and truly? Why must her heart cry out for a man who was a libertine, and whose rank must ever be a barrier between them?

That night her dreams were wild and frightening, and she awoke feeling unrefreshed and with shadows under her eyes and declined to go driving with her sisters. But when John Hillier called, she went riding with him, hoping that a brisk gallop in the fresh air would revive her spirits. She was careful not to speak of Elise, but John did.

'I saw no reason to attend upon Madame de la Fournes last night,' he remarked, frowning. 'She had no vapours and had expressed no wish for me to escort her to Cavendish Square. 'Twas all a trick of Mademoiselle Elise. You had left before I discovered it, else I would have refused.'

'Oh, you could not have done that,' Prue said quickly. 'They are the Duke's family and he is your employer. It would have been very unwise for you to displease Mademoiselle Elise.'

His mouth tightened, but he said no more. The Courtney carriage came past and Prue rode up to greet the family. Hester leaned forward, smiling as she said,

'Do you see the *Morning Post* this morning? There is a pretty remark about three angelic creatures who came to earth last night at Almack's. It is written in sweet style! I congratulate you and your sisters.'

Mrs Courtney added her congratulations and invited Prue and her companion to return with them and take mid-morning refreshment. Prue, glad of anything which would keep her uneasy thoughts at bay, accepted.

There was a gay company at the Courtney residence, and soon Prue found herself parted from John and being offered a glass of negus by the Courtney cousin, Richard Unwin, as portentous and heavily gallant as ever.

'I am informed you and your charming sisters were excessively admired last night,' he said, bowing. 'But 'tis not to be wondered at, if I may be allowed to say so.'

'Oh yes, you may most certainly say so,' Prue told him mischievously, 'if you do not mind trifling with the truth.'

'Oh, I am ever concerned with truth,' he protested. 'In fact, I shall reveal a truth to you which is just come about. Miss Minnie has honoured me by accepting my offer of marriage!'

'Then I congratulate you most heartily, and wish you every happiness.'

He bowed again, and spent some time discoursing gravely on his expectations of happiness in the married state. Later, Prue found Minnie and offered good wishes for her future happiness.

'Richard has a kind heart, 'tis why I accepted him,' Minnie said with unexpected frankness. 'Mama is all for his fortune and estates in Sussex, but I would not have taken him had I not known he had good sense and sobriety, and would not tease me.'

'Not exactly a romantic approach to matrimony,' Prue murmured to Hester later, 'but many successful marriages have been built upon less.'

John rode back with her to Grosvenor Street. He had said no word of when the Duke was expected, and Prue had not the courage to ask. She found a note from Elise awaiting her.

'Sweetest friend' she read, 'I implore you to visit me! Let us gossip and talk scandal and amuse ourselves. I find most English females sadly without spirit. Do not disappoint me, I beg.'

So Elise had forgiven her, Prue thought happily. She was like a child with her sudden moods, a butterfly who was never poised for long on one spot.

She was smiling as she went upstairs to the drawing-room. As she entered, a sturdy, plainly-dressed young man rose from his chair and Selina cried,

'La, sister, such a surprise! Here's Jim come to see how we do in London!'

Prue looked at Selina's flushed cheeks and dancing eyes and grasped the hand Jim held out, saying, 'Indeed, there is no one more welcome! Come, Jim, you must tell us all of what goes at home, how dear Papa was when you left, and of your new house and lands . . . and how many hunters you have bought since we left Northumberland!'

His hand tightened on hers as he looked at her hard.

'Aye, I shall tell all I know, Mistress Prue, but first I'm saying "thank you".'

'Why in the world do you thank her?' Selina demanded, looking from one to the other in puzzlement.

Jim smiled and released Prue's hand. 'Your sister knows—and Sir Roland. Maybe I'll tell you one day, Miss Selina.'

Cassie came to Prue's room that night.

'Mama is in a fine fit of the sullens,' she said. ''Tis no part of her plans to see Selina wed to a country squire.'

'But Selina has ever had a feeling for Jim, I think. Perhaps her unfortunate infatuation for Sir Joseph showed her where her heart lay,' Prue said as she brushed her thick, curly hair.

Cassie wandered to the door. 'I wonder what brought Jim to think of coming to London? He hates cities.'

''Tis a mystery,' Prue agreed, and turned away to hide her smile.

# CHAPTER SIXTEEN

ELISE sent her mother's carriage for Prue. Madame da la Fournes was no longer staying at the Duke's residence, but had taken a house in Bond Street where she planned to entertain. When the girls met, Elise was sweetly affectionate and full of congratulations on Prue's success at the assembly.

'We must see much of each other,' Elise declared gaily. 'Mama will be entertaining for me, and I shall *insist* you are invited. Now you must tell me something.' She slipped her arm through Prue's as they walked into the pretty little parlour. 'Who is your favourite beau? You have broken many hearts—oh yes, I am sure of it! You must have a *tendresse* for one special gentleman, is it not so? When am I to congratulate on your engagement to some handsome lord?'

'Indeed you must wait, I fear,' Prue said, laughing, 'for I have attached no gentleman seriously.'

'You have not secured anyone yet?' Elise looked at her a trifle sharply. 'But does not your excellent Mama arrange a marriage for you? You have been in London for some time, have you not? It is strange.'

'It would be stranger if I allowed my mother to choose a husband for me,' Prue assured her.

'And still you have not chosen?' Elise sank into a chair. 'There is no one in love with you?'

Prue hesitated. John Hillier, she knew, was in love with her, but remembering what she had observed at Almack's, she said lightly, 'No one has yet declared himself, I fear.'

Was there a look of relief on Elise's charming face? If so, it was gone before Prue could decide.

'But of course you will marry soon.' Elise turned as a footman brought in a tray with lemonade, cakes and fruit. 'Now tell me how I looked at Almack's. Did you like my gown? John said I made other girls look *très ordinaire!*' She laughed as she poured out lemonade for her friend.

They proceeded to gossip pleasantly. Elise had a sharp eye and a caustic tongue and her remarks on London society, if unkind, were often very shrewd. Suddenly she said,

'John tells me Charles is come to Cavendish Square.'

Prue felt her heart leap and was unhappily aware Elise had seen the quick colour that rose in her face.

'Oh, is he? I suppose Abbotstone became too dull for him when all his guests left,' she said, looking down at the glass she held.

'Charles is not happy unless he is in London chasing some pretty woman. But of course you know that! He tried to make love to *you*, in the library at Abbotstone, did he not?' She laughed. 'You were not pleased, I think, my sweet Prue.' Her face changed suddenly. 'It would indeed be very terrible if you should like Charles too much. He is attractive, oh yes, but he does not have a heart that is faithful. I think perhaps he has no heart, poor Charles, he seeks only pretty women to amuse him.'

'He does not, then, wish to marry?' Prue raised her eyes to see Elise smiling.

'Oh yes, Charles will marry one day; he will take some very grand lady with *généalogie* as long as his own.'

Prue was silent. It was what she had always known. Any other marriage was impossible for such a man.

"*Ma chérie*, forgive me if I say you should not meet my naughty Charles again.' Prue started and caught her breath. 'I think perhaps you do like him just a little too much, but you must forget him, put him away from your thoughts. He will be very charming to you because you are pretty, but . . .' Elise bent forward, putting her hand on Prue's, 'I think it is best that you shall go away for a while, perhaps, to return to your home in the north. If you should fall too deeply in love with Charles——'

'Elise, what silly notion is this?' Prue said sharply. 'You will provoke me if you continue to speak so.'

'Oh, I would not wish that, sweet friend! I wanted to warn you——'

'I need no warning. Come, let us see the patterns you have for your new gown.'

The pleasure in her visit had gone, Prue found, and she left as soon as she could. Was it possible that she had given herself away to Elise? The thought distressed her for some time until she reminded herself of her friend's butterfly mind. Elise knew Charles' charm, and had meant only to warn. She could not know of what had passed between her cousin and her 'sweet friend'.

But the Duke was in London, and perhaps he would call at Grosvenor Street and she would have to receive him. Oh, surely she would be strong enough to crush this disastrous infatuation—for it must be that—which he had inspired in her? He had insulted her beyond forgiveness! He had cruelly awakened her to passion! He had earned her contempt. She must learn to hate him!

Lady Angel made it very plain that she considered Jim West's arrival an impertinence. She ignored him when he called and lost her temper with Selina.

'I do not care a fig!' Selina declared to her sisters. 'She's in a fit of the sullens because I like Jim better than the primpish young bucks I've met here! I know I can trust Jim, and she's quite out if she thinks I shall give him up!'

'Are you so taken with him then, after your ill-treatment of him?' Cassie asked.

Selina smiled and turned away without answering. Prue,

watching her, knew she had done the right thing in suggesting to her father that Selina was missing Jim. Her sister's first burst of enthusiasm for London society and flirting had been killed by her unfortunate involvement with Sir Joseph. Jim would make a loving and faithful husband, and would be undisturbed by her shallow and unthinking nature.

Mrs Beauford was busy receiving congratulations from her friends on having obtained good settlements for her daughters. Lady Angel became vapourish and was not at home to her dear Dorcas when she called.

'She comes to put me to the blush because none of you has found a husband,' she complained to Prue. 'I take it very unkindly.'

'You *could* say Selina has a devoted admirer in Jim,' Prue suggested mischievously.

'That creature? I would be ashamed to own it!'

'Papa thinks well of Jim, he has told me so. Now that Jim has an estate and a comfortable income, he is quite a catch.'

'Selina shall not waste herself upon him,' her mother snapped. 'Leave me alone, my head aches quite abominably! Send Lizzie to me, and tell James I shall see no one today.'

'Why, then, that's a pity,' Cassie said gaily, putting her head round the door. 'I'll advise the Duke you've a migraine and——'

'The Duke?' Lady Angel gasped, spilling the cup of lemon-water she had been sipping. 'Oh, dear heaven! Don't let him go . . . Prue . . . Cassie . . . Lizzie—where is the wretch? I'll dress at once! Go to him, daughters, and say I'll attend him immediately!'

Prue had subdued her first agitation by the time she entered the drawing-room, and was able to meet the Duke with a tranquillity she was far from feeling. He greeted her with his usual urbane courtesy, but she saw the sudden light in his eyes and turned away swiftly.

'I trust your visit to Dorset was beneficial—' he was

beginning, when James announced Madame de la Fournes and her daughter.

Elise's eyes widened. 'La, Charles, I thought you were to drive in the park this morning.' She looked around the room. 'Is John with you?'

'He comes betimes,' her cousin told her, 'and I beg you will not attach him for some fribble, he has work to do for me.'

'Alas, poor John! You are a driver of slaves, Charles.'

Soon after this Lady Angel made her appearance, slightly breathless from being laced into her gown so hurriedly, and full of apologies and offers of refreshments. Without quite knowing how, Prue found herself alone with the Duke in a corner of the room. He stood staring down at her, frowning, while she sought for words to cover her rising agitation. Suddenly he said, startling her by the harshness of his voice,

'Prue, how long will you keep me in suspense? You have a feeling for me, I know I am right. You cannot for ever stand out against me. You are not so cool as you pretend.' He caught her hand, laying a finger on her wrist. 'Your pulse races . . . and your colour rises!'

She tore her hand away and stepped back. 'I have told you I shall never, *never* become another of your loves!' His touch had set her nerves afire and she was trembling.

'There are not many now,' he murmured, his eyes on her averted face. 'You are taking too large a place in my life, Prue. I mean to have you.'

She could not speak. Her heart was racing unevenly, making her feel faint. A terrible weakness came over her, sweeping away all her resolutions to hate and despise this man who had so powerful a hold upon her heart. For she knew, with sudden, blinding certainty, that she loved him, and this love had been steadily growing within her until she could no longer refuse to acknowledge it.

But he would never know! She would fight with all her strength to overcome this shameful weakness, this passion for a man who could be her ruin. To surrender to him was an ecstasy she would never know. From somewhere she would find courage to resist and fortitude to live without his love.

An exclamation from Elise gave her the excuse to slip away. John Hillier had entered the room and Elise was upbraiding him for being late. John smiled, and turned to Prue to ask if she intended to ride in the park that afternoon.

Elise laid her hand on Prue's arm and said swiftly: 'No, she comes with me to the shops! You shall not steal her from me, John! We must see what style the new bonnets take, must we not?' She turned a smiling face to Prue, who looked surprised as she murmured,

'I did not know we had arranged . . . But yes, of course, Elise, if you wish me to go with you.'

'Then tomorrow,' John said with determination. He did not look at Elise. 'I shall call in the morning, with your permission.'

Prue felt Elise's hand tighten on her arm before falling away.

'*I* shall learn to ride,' Elise said lightly,' you shall teach me, John.'

Making the excuse that she must attend her other guests, Prue moved away. Something in the little scene disturbed her. It would be unfortunate if Elise had truly fallen in love with John; Madame de la Fournes would certainly not allow a marriage with someone so unimportant as John. She had a sudden longing to get away, to be by herself and let her taut nerves relax, to stop thinking, feeling . . . She remembered Elise's advice. Would it be best to return to Northumberland? To remove herself from temptation?

A new, disquieting thought struck her: had Elise's suggestion to do with John and not the Duke? Had she guessed John's feelings for her friend, and wished her out of the way?

Lady Angel was in high delight after the company had left. The Duke had mentioned an entertainment at Ranelagh, and

Madame de la Fournes had been most gracious.

'But I still say I cannot think much of her daughter,' she remarked. 'She is vastly over-dressed, and too free in her manners.'

'It is odd she changed her mind so abruptly,' Cassie said thoughtfully. 'A few minutes before she said Prue was to shop with her this afternoon, she had told me she had an engagement for a concert.'

Prue sighed. It would sadden her if a misunderstanding should cloud her friendship with pretty, lively little Elise, who had professed such friendship for her.

'Even if I persuade her I have no attachment for John,' she thought, 'she may guess he feels some tenderness for me, and it will cause her unhappiness.'

How complicated her life had become since leaving her home. Her father's words came back to her with unhappy distinctness as she sat alone in her room looking out at the sunlit street: 'You will meet many men, few of whom you can trust. . . . I tremble for you, Prue. . . .'

After the shopping trip, Prue did not see Elise for some days. Madame de la Fournes was busy with preparations for a ball to launch her daughter in society and as yet Prue had not received an invitation. It did not trouble her. She was feeling restless and had no desire for society. Her mother remarked on her low spirits, and she was made to swallow a herbal tonic and ordered to bed early.

His Grace the Duke had called twice but she had avoided him, and she attended only such entertainments where she was fairly sure of not meeting him.

She was busy one morning, writing her weekly letter to her father, when Cassie came into the room looking grave, and sank into a chair.

''Pon honour, there's little peace in this house now! Mama has just given Selina a fine wigging for seeing so much of poor

Jim.'

Prue put down her pen. 'Mama is wrong. Jim is trustworthy and has true affection for Selina and she has discovered she likes him.'

'Oh, she dotes upon him! I find him somewhat boring, but she is in the way of losing her heart entirely.'

'Is she much upset?'

Cassie frowned slightly. 'She was somewhat strange. She smiled and was as quiet as a mouse—which ain't her way, as you know.' She looked at Prue. 'Mama had best be careful, I think. She doesn't understand Selina . . . she doesn't understand any of us, Prue. And Mama has changed since coming to London.'

'We have all changed,' Prue said quietly, resting her head upon her hand. 'I wonder if we were wise to come.'

Cassie jumped up. 'Oh, we would have grown mould if we'd stayed at home—and I wouldn't have met Harry.' She laughed. 'Poor Mama! Not one of us has caught a rich nobleman! She thinks Aunt Fanny's money perfectly wasted!'

Prue was not surprised when Selina declined to leave her room. She saw to it that supper was brought to her sister, despite Lady Angel's orders to the contrary.

'Starvation will soon bring her to her right mind,' Lady Angel stated grimly, 'and we'll have no more of this boorish fellow and ideas that she loves him. She nearly ruined herself once. . . .'

'But this is different,' Prue protested. 'Jim is a good, steady man and——'

'And he will *not* marry my daughter!' Lady Angel's colour was dangerously high and her eyes angry. 'Hold your peace, chit! *I* decide such questions!'

Instructions were given to the servants that Mr Jim West was to be refused admittance. Lady Angel, driven into a frenzy of irritation by her friend Dorcas's complacent triumph, determined to tighten her hold upon her daughters.

Prue was in her bedroom unwrapping the fan she had bought that day—she had put the Duke's fan away; she would not use anything that could remind her of him—when Mollie knocked and entered, looking troubled and uncertain.

'Well Mollie, what is it?' Prue smiled at the little maid who had become her devoted attendant.

'I—I'm not oversure, Mistress Prue. I'm not one as wishes to make trouble and . . . I know 'tis no matter of mine, but . . .' she twisted her apron and then went on with a rush: ''Tis Miss Selina! She ain't in her room—nor nowhere in the house.'

Prue let the fan slip from her fingers as she stared at the girl.

'Not *again*? Pray heaven she has done nothing rash! Mollie, say nothing of this to anyone.'

'Oh no, miss, I never would! She's took some of her things with her just like before!'

Prue left her and went down the stairs slowly, wondering how best to break it to her mother. This time there was no one to help them. As she came in sight of the hall she saw the footman at the door, having just taken something from a messenger.

'A letter for her ladyship,' he said, and gave it to her.

Cassie, who had joined Prue, exclaimed, 'It is in Selina's hand. But how . . .'

'She's gone,' Prue said. 'Come, we must give this to Mama at once.'

Lady Angel's face expressed nothing but peevish resentment.

'No doubt the naughty chit has run off to friends and writes me in defiance. I'll soon have her back, and she shall be locked in her room this time.'

She opened the note and Prue watched the colour drain from her face and her chin begin to tremble.

'*No!* It *cannot* be! I will not believe it. . . . She could not be so mad! After all I've done for her . . .'

'Mama, what is it?' Prue begged. 'What does she tell you?'

'She—she's *married* the wretched man! Oh, my heart! My poor nerves! It will be the death of me, I know! When your poor father knows of this——'

'When Papa knows I believe he'll give his blessing,' Cassie declared firmly. 'He has always liked Jim.'

'But Selina is not of age,' Prue put in anxiously. 'Such a marriage, without parental consent, may not be valid.'

A shriek from her mother startled both girls.

'Oh, dear heaven! She is gone with him unwed! She is ruined indeed! Wicked, wicked creature. . . .'

'And who, pray, is this wicked creature?' a voice behind them asked calmly.

Prue whirled around, hardly daring to believe her ears. Then she ran forward joyously.

'Papa! Oh, you have come! How *good* it is to see you! When did you arrive? Why did you not tell us? Why——'

'Peace, child—and do not attempt to strangle me, I pray. I cannot answer all questions at once. I must greet your mother.'

Lady Angel rose and cast herself into his arms, wailing.

'Oh, husband! Such a disaster! Such shame brought upon us by your wicked daughter . . . and this time no hope of rescuing her! She is lost to us!'

'La, Mama, don't put yourself in such a tweak.' Selina, on the arm of a joyously smiling Jim, entered. 'You've achieved a married daughter at last. Ain't you proud?'

'And married with her father's consent,' Sir Roland stated firmly. 'The feather-brained little creature had the sense to choose a husband who will put up with her—and keep her in order. Let me hear no more wailing and talk of ruin. Where is James?'

'Here, sir, and very gratified to see you again, sir.'

'Yes, yes. Well bring us wine, James, we celebrate a

wedding.'

Prue gently straightened her mother's cap. 'Dear Mama, pray consider. I do not believe Minnie Beauford's Richard has any better estate and fortune than Jim.'

Her mother stared, sighed and brightened. 'Why, now you say it, 'tis quite possible . . . and Jim is a sight better-looking than poor Richard!'

# CHAPTER SEVENTEEN

FACED with the inevitable, Lady Angel accepted Selina's marriage to Jim with better grace than her family expected. She busied herself buying Selina wedding clothes.

''Tis a trifle late, of course,' she grumbled, 'but you shall not take your place in northern society without a proper wardrobe.'

Once that was accomplished, she invited her dear friend, Dorcas Beauford, to visit her and Prue had difficulty in hiding her amusement at her mother's highflown description of Jim's estates, and Selina's luck in finding so desirable a husband.

''Fore God, there's not a miss in the county that isn't after Jim,' Lady Angel told her friend as they sat over a cup of tea. 'But it was always Selina he fancied. He pursued her to London, and she finally decided to have him.'

'I'm sure I congratulate you, Clarissa.' Mrs Beauford, from her exalted position of mother of *two* engaged daughters, could afford to be generous. 'He seems a fine young man. But why the secret wedding?'

Lady Angel was prepared for that. 'Oh, la! Selina is the most romantic of creatures! She had some silly notion I might think her too young to wed and would make her wait a year, and she let Jim persuade her to elope! She even coaxed her father to come and give his sanction. I should scold the little wretch, but she is in such a swoon of love and happiness I do not have the heart!'

'A most notable performance,' Cassie whispered in Prue's

ear, 'I vow Mrs Siddons should look to her laurels!'

Neither of the newlyweds wished to remain in London. Sir Roland confessed to Prue that, glad as he was to be reunited with his family—and most particularly with her—he found the city affecting his health, and greatly missed the tranquillity of his home in the north.

'So I shall accompany your sister and my son-in-law back to Northumberland,' he said. He looked across the breakfast table at Prue. 'And what of you, child? Have you wearied yet of the delights of smart society? Would you not like a respite from your mother's reproaches at your failure to catch a titled and wealthy husband? I miss you, daughter.'

She put her hand quickly over his, pressing it as she said warmly, 'Indeed, sir, I have missed you greatly too. But since Mama is set to remain here for the rest of the season, and Cassie has no wish to leave . . .'

'Because of some young sprig your mother has no wish to see her marry,' Sir Roland finished for her. He sighed. 'I find such ambition, such seeking after false values, fatiguing. Well, if you will not come with me I must leave you either to satisfy your mother's hopes or endure her reproaches.'

Selina could not be gone soon enough. She was wild to take her place as Jim's wife in his new house, and show off her London gowns and talk of her social successes with her friends. Except for losing her father's society, Prue was glad when they had gone and the house could settle down after all the bustle and upset.

She had seen nothing of Elise or John. But some days later she was in the stillroom when the footman came to say there were guests arriving, and she hurried to the drawing-room. As she opened the door she heard Cassie saying: 'Oh yes, we had much excitement, and my sister is gone back to Northumberland.'

'La, I am desolate!' Elise's light voice answered. 'How I shall miss her charming company.'

Prue entered and curtsied to Madame de la Fournes and Mrs Courtney who sat with her mother. She saw Elise turn her head and heard her quick intake of breath.

'*Tiens*! I thought your sister said you were gone away . . .' she paused, biting her lip.

'Oh, 'twas Selina who went north,' Cassie said. 'You'll be pleased to know it was not Prue, I'll wager.'

'But of *course* I am enchanted that my dearest Prue is still with us.' Elise came up and caught Prue's hand. 'I *was* surprised,' she whispered. 'I thought you had taken my advice and flown from *him*! It would have been wiser, sweet friend. Something has happened . . . it would indeed be wise for you to leave London now.'

'What is your meaning, pray?' Prue asked, astonished. 'What has happened?'

'Oh I cannot tell you now, but it is not good and I am very much overset! When we are alone I shall tell you. . . . Ah, John comes! He has promised to teach me to ride, so I may ride with him in the park. He greatly wishes it, you know.' She flitted away from Prue.

For a moment Prue felt uneasy, then she remembered her friend's habit of exaggeration and love of making much of small matters. She turned to find Hester at her side.

'I have not seen you this age, Prue. This is fine news about Selina. To marry for love is so much better than seeking wealth and a fine social position. She has more sensibility than I suspected.'

'Indeed, I rejoice for her, she is very happy,' Prue said, taking her friend's arm. 'Hester, cannot you stay with us for the afternoon? I would dearly like it.'

Mrs Courtney, when approached, gave her permission. John Hillier, standing near, turned to Prue.

'The day is fine; perhaps you and Mistress Courtney would consider a walk in the park? I would be honoured if I might accompany you.'

'No, no, John,' Elise caught his arm. 'I have perfectly forgotten to tell you! Charles wishes you to attend upon Mama and me when we visit the Tower Zoo this afternoon. Mama is vastly interested in wild beasts, and Charles does not wish us to go unattended.'

John frowned impatiently. 'He said nothing of this to me.'

'*Ma foi*! Charles forgets much when he is interested in . . . other affairs.' She sent a swift glance to Prue. 'Mama shall send the carriage for you.'

Prue turned away, and with her arm in Hester's went into the adjoining room where refreshments had been laid out. Hester drew her to one side.

'Prue, I pray I do not hurt you when I say I do not care overmuch for your little French miss. She is very charming and pretty, but I feel I would not greatly trust her. I know you are fond of her, but—forgive me—I am not persuaded she has much love for you. And it is patent that she is jealous because Mr Hillier shows preference for you.'

Prue sighed, and admitted she had been disturbed by Elise's attempts to attach John and her suspicion that John resented it.

'If she is sincerely attached to him,' she said, 'I fear she will be unhappy. But she is light-hearted and perhaps does not have such deep emotions as I think, and will soon find another handsome young beau to take her attention. Indeed I hope so.'

Hester shook her head. 'I wonder.'

Cassie came into the room with Harry. 'Oh, Prue, Mama and Mrs Courtney have such an idea! It is beyond anything delightful! There is to be a most fine river entertainment next week on barges, with music and singing by the Italian prima donna! All London will be there.'

Hester smiled. 'Then every barge on the river will be required.'

'It promises to be a very fine affair,' Harry told her. 'If the weather will stay as warm and clear as it is now, it will make a splendid spectacle. The barges are to be splendidly decorated and moored in mid-stream.'

'And Mama is all for taking us!' Cassie's blue eyes sparkled. 'I pray it will be warm, and I need not wear a pelisse and so hide my Italian silk! It is so vastly modish and I wish all the *ton* to see it!'

When they returned to the drawing-room they found that Madame de la Fournes and her daughter had departed, taking John with them. Lady Angel and Mrs Courtney were discussing arrangements for the river party, a discussion that carried them up to the hour for dinner.

Despite the unhappiness of her feeling for the man whose image haunted her, and her uneasiness over Elise's curious behaviour, Prue was caught up in the excitement of preparing for the evening on the river. The Beaufords were joining their party, and several other friends including—despite Lady Angel's coldness at the suggestion—Harry. A special landing stage had been built for the embarkation and the Signorina was said to be in fine voice, and Cassie's fears that her Italian gown would not be noticed were stilled when the evening proved warm and fine.

Prue could not help wondering if the Duke would grace the occasion with his presence. He had not called again, and Elise did not mention him and had said nothing further of the 'something' which had happened that made it necessary for her friend to leave the city.

A cloudless sky in which stars began to glitter arched over the convoy of elegant coaches, chaises and landaus that converged upon the wooden landing stage hung with flags and coloured lanterns that sent fingers of light upon the dark waters.

The barges moored alongside were splendidly set with banks of flowers, velvet drapes and rich carpets. An orchestra was ensconced on a floating platform hung with swags of coloured silk, and all was illuminated with tiny fairy lights swaying gently in the breeze.

Prue felt her heart lift as she looked at the enchanting and romantic scene. The women, powdered and scented, their rich satins and brocades rustling as they stepped from their coaches, their jewels catching the light as, with fans fluttering, they were escorted on to the barges by gentlemen hardly less gorgeously attired.

Lady Angel was all fuss and apprehension lest they should be relegated to some inconspicuous position. She was determined that she and her daughters should be seen and, for once, was glad of Harry's gentle but firm insistence on the barge master's placing them in a good position.

'La, there is the Countess of Longworthy,' Lady Angel bowed graciously, 'and Sir Roderick. . . . And I vow that wicked creature, Miss Granton, has the face to appear with her new lover! Pray, Prue, is my head in order? Does the feather slip?'

Prue assured her mother that her elaborate head arrangement was in order, and proceeded to look around her. Voices arose on either side, gay voices exchanging greetings and sallies. Suddenly she felt her heart jolt in her breast and for a second the bright scene swam before her eyes as a voice, assured and somewhat arrogant, spoke behind her.

'I am enchanted, Lady Angel, to find you here with your daughters.'

Prue did not turn her head until she felt her mother tug at the skirts of her white brocade gown and whisper, 'Prue! *Prue*! Here is His Grace the Duke most kindly addressing us. Are you deaf, daughter?'

Prue turned her head slowly. Her breath caught in her throat as she met the mocking grey eyes of the Duke of Carlington. He was in his favourite grey velvet, his hair lightly powdered and delicate lace at his throat and wrist. He bowed.

'We have many beauties with us tonight, but i'faith, Mistress Prue, you outshine them all. A white rose, cool, mysterious, lovely.'

She raised her fan to hide the sudden trembling of her lips. She would not for the world have him know how his presence disturbed her. Pride came to her rescue and she said evenly,

'A most graceful compliment, sir. But 'tis commonly known that you are master of such elegant flattery.'

''Tis no flattery, I vow.' He moved nearer and a dashing young blade in purple satin hastily gave up his seat at a meaning glance from His Grace's eyes. 'I have not seen you lately, but it is no mystery.' He bent nearer, his eyes on her averted face. 'I find you disturb my peace of mind, Prue, and life without peace of mind is not to my liking. So . . . I have not sought you out, as perhaps you have noticed.'

She looked at him, her chin high and her eyes dark and cool.

'Indeed, sir, I have been too busy to notice such a disaster. My father has been with us, and my sister is lately married.'

'Ah yes, the pretty runaway.' He opened his snuffbox and took a pinch, looking thoughtful. 'Did she choose to elope this time?'

'Well. . . .' Against her will, Prue laughed. 'I fear she did not tell us of her intention, but my father knew and attended the ceremony.'

'I am happy to hear it. I trust her husband will beat her if she ever feels the inclination to run away again.' He glanced down at the fan she held. 'I see you do not honour me by using my fan.'

'No,' her voice was steady despite the quick beating of her heart under the satin of her bodice, 'I prefer this one.'

He was silent so long that she was forced to look up at him, and found his eyes fixed upon her with something in them that set her blood pounding in her veins. He said softly.

'It will do you no good, Prue, you shall not escape me. You

do not hate me—or despise me. No, no matter how you protest. I do not intend to keep away again. You were made for love, my beautiful, tantalizing Prue, *my* love!'

For a second she could not tear her eyes away from his. Her fingers closed upon her fragile fan in an endeavour to still their trembling. Suddenly the slender sticks snapped, and the Duke's smile brought a wave of hot colour to her face as he gently removed the broken fan from her hand.

'I shall keep this, my sweet Prue. It tells me you are afraid . . . of yourself as well as of me! Do not deny it! You are a disruptive influence on my life, Prue; I am gratified by observing I have something of the same influence on yours.'

'You are mistaken, sir.' Anger rose above her distress as she returned his gaze squarely. 'You are so assured of your success with my sex that you do not recognise and will not accept defeat! I have *no* feeling for you, beyond gratitude for what you did to save my sister from her rashness; that, I shall always remember. Could you forget this—this unseemly passion, I would value your friendship.'

'I have no wish for your friendship!' The violence of his voice startled her and she drew back, catching her breath as she saw the blaze lighting his eyes. 'Do not dare to use that word with me.'

He stopped abruptly as a hand fell upon his shoulder and a languid young gentleman whose eyes rested admiringly on Prue, drawled, 'A thousand pardons, Charles, but your estimable aunt, Lady Anne Bouchier, sends me to demand that you attend upon her. She is in some tweak about her seat and says the lanterns will set fire to her hair, I believe.'

The Duke rose with an impatient exclamation. 'If it were paradise itself my good aunt would find fault with it!' He bowed stiffly and made his way through the brilliant throng.

Prue watched him go, knowing that all her pleasure in the evening had flown. To realise he felt passion for her, that he found her beautiful and desirable, that he had not been able to keep away from her, was a most painful joy, and she shivered when she thought of his words. But his passion was dishonourable, and she should find no joy in it if she had any pride.

# CHAPTER EIGHTEEN

THE scene was a brilliant one. The barges with their golden lights rocked gently on the dark water, music and the silver voice of the great Italian soprano floated up into the soft night sky. Servants brought food and wine to the dazzling company as they laughed and flirted and whispered behind delicate fans. But none of the evening's beauty touched Prue as she sat staring with unseeing eyes across the river. The Duke's words had stirred unknown emotions deep within her, and she was having difficulty in composing herself so that her mother and friends would not observe her agitation.

Suddenly she heard Cassie exclaim: 'Why, here comes Mademoiselle Elise. Her gown is very charming but la!— so many frills and flounces hung on it! It would set me in a tweak to manage them all!'

It was indeed Elise, dressed in violet brocade, who was threading her way through the crowd, her expressive little face alight with pleasure as she nodded and waved to acquaintances. She sank, panting, into a seat beside Prue and fanned herself vigorously.

'Or, heaven! I am a nymph pursued, my sweet Prue! A young lord—*un beau monsieur*—teases me to death, so I escape him and come to your party.' She turned her head to stare around her.

'Then we must find you a protector,' Prue said, smiling. 'John will challenge him to a duel!'

The fluttering fan stilled for a second. 'You expect John?' Elise asked sharply.

'Oh no, but I think I saw him as we arrived.'

'And you think he will seek you out?'

'Of course not,' Prue said hastily. 'Why should I?'

'Because, perhaps, you think he is a little devoted to you?'

'You talk nonsense, Elise,' Prue rebuked her lightly, but she felt uncomfortable under her friend's steady gaze. 'John has been kind to us and we are all grateful to him. He is a good friend to me.'

Elise closed her fan slowly, her eyes lowered until the long lashes swept her cheeks as she said softly, 'I am glad. Then he will not be distressed when you leave London.'

'But I have not yet decided . . .' Prue began quickly, then paused, struck by something in Elise's face. A sudden premonition of disaster caught and chilled her. She leaned forward. 'Elise, what is it? What has happened that causes you to insist I must leave London? You promised to tell me.'

Lady Angel had moved away to talk to a friend and the girls were for the moment alone. Elise raised her eyes, and her small hand caught Prue's arm as she whispered,

'Oh, my dearest friend! How can I say it? When first I hear it I think—but *no*! It *cannot* be true, it is a wicked rumour! So I wait to hear more. Now I am certain! It is spoken of freely—yet with discretion so *you* shall not hear it! But you will hear whispers, yes, and see sly smiles and observe how the women titter and the men grow familiar. . . . Oh! That he could do such a thing! To try to smirch your reputation so! Indeed he is truly the Perfidious Devil!'

For a moment Prue could not speak. An icy hand seemed to grip her heart. At last she managed to whisper, 'Elise, tell me *at once* what you mean! What has your cousin the Duke done or said that makes you speak so?'

Elise's hand tightened on Prue's arm. 'Yes, you must know, it is right you shall know so you can escape him! Charles has made a wager with Lord Barony that he will seduce you. That you will become his new light of love! That you will be ruined beyond help! Alas, all London knows of it—and waits for the Perfidious Devil to win his horrid wager!'

For a second the bright light whirled in a dizzying arc around Prue, and she felt deadly faint. She shut her eyes, willing herself to calmness. It could not be true! The Duke was known as a libertine, but he was a man of the first rank and he would not, could not, stoop to such evil! That he desired her, she knew, but to plan to ruin her for a wager, a wager made with the notorious lecher Lord Barony . . .

'I do not believe it!' She looked at Elise's distressed face. 'He would not . . . You have been misled.'

'Alas! 'Tis but too true, dear Prue! And it makes me weep with shame for him. He is determined to have you! Oh—these wicked men! Now you will see why you must go away from London *at once*. He will not pursue you once you are under your father's roof. Prue, I implore you not to wait until you succumb, I know you are not indifferent to him . . .'

She turned her head sharply, her expression altering in a flash. 'Ah John! You look for me I think. Now you can take me back to Mama and stop that stupid little beau from teasing me further.' She rose in a swirl of violet brocade and fluttering lace. As she moved past Prue she bent and whispered: 'My dearest friend, I have greatly distressed you, but it is right that you shall know your danger. Go back to Northumberland, I beg of you, *chérie*! I am friendly with Lord Barony's sister—she is a sad gossip—and it is she who tells me of this dreadful wickedness. Go, before all London rings with the Devil's wager!'

The music, the laughter and light voices, the gentle lapping of water against the barges faded and for a blinding moment Prue saw nothing but a handsome, arrogant face and a pair of grey eyes ablaze with passion and heard again a man's fierce whisper: 'I am not a man to be thwarted! You shall be mine, willing or unwilling!'

'Prue, dear,' Cassie had dropped into the seat Elise had vacated, 'are you taken faint? You look vastly pale. Mama has a vinaigrette ...'

'Say nothing to her,' Prue murmured quickly. 'I—perhaps it is the motion of the water.... I shall recover immediately. If you will lend me your fan, Cassie ...'

Cassie said no more, but she managed to extract her mother's vinaigrette from her reticule without that good lady noticing it. She whispered a command to Harry, who was never far from her side, and he disappeared and came back with a glass of Malaga which Prue accepted gratefully.

With a surge of relief, Prue noticed that people were beginning to move, and the barges were slowly returning to the landing stage. Thank God! The evening was nearly over! She must keep up the appearance of tranquillity a little longer until she could be alone with this horror. He was a devil indeed, who could so callously wreck a woman's honour! If her father should ever know.... Prue shivered, although the night was still warm.

All became bustle and confusion. Coaches drove up, horses snorted, whips cracked and voices were raised, calling coachmen, bidding farewells and complaining of delays. As the crowd surged forward to disembark, Prue found herself forced to one side and away from her party. She waited, unwilling to push her way through the noisy crowd, shrinking from what she might see in their eyes or hear in their amused whispers. Was all London aware of her shame? Were other wagers being taken among the rakish young bucks on the Perfidious Devil's chance of success?

And this was the man she could not tear from her heart, whom she feared because of her own treacherous weakness.

She stood by the side of the barge staring down at the lapping water, seeing and hearing nothing. Suddenly a voice made her start violently.

'Mistress Prue, your family and their party have already

departed, their coach being overfull. Your mother has most graciously given me her consent to offer you my escort and carriage to take you to Grosvenor Street.'

She turned slowly, trying to control the sudden trembling that seized her. He was regarding her with a faint smile, urbane, cool, assured as he offered her his arm.

'I fear I must refuse your offer, sir.' To her great relief her voice held no hint of her inner agitation. 'If my family is gone, I shall take a hackney.'

'I fear you will be unlucky. 'Tis grown late, and all available hired coaches are taken. See, we are almost the last to leave.'

It was true. She had not realised how long she had stood wrapped in her thoughts while the crowds had driven off in their own coaches or hired hackneys. Only a few figures lingered on the wharf and there was no sign of any vehicle.

'Come, Prue,' the Duke's voice was imperative. 'You shall come with me. Your mother——'

'My mother has an unfortunate misunderstanding of your character, sir.' Prue, some measure of her self-confidence returning, faced him squarely. 'I do not wish you to escort me home.'

The corners of his mouth twitched. 'Then may I ask how you intend to return to Grosvenor Street? 'Tis a fine night, I allow, but to walk . . . and in such dainty shoes . . .'

She bit her lip. It was true that there seemed no chance of hiring a carriage, and already there were gathered along the river banks some dark and shabby figures shuffling past with furtive eyes on the alert, the miserable night creatures who prowled the city, a threat to lonely travellers.

The Duke's hand was upon her arm, a firm hand brooking no opposition. Unwillingly, unable to refuse, she went with him and saw his handsome coach drive up out of the shadows. Her heart was beating almost to suffocate her as he opened the door and she was forced to step in. Now she was lost! How could her mother be so obtuse, so wickedly blind and stupid not to realise such a man's intentions? In spite of all warnings, Lady Angel persisted in hoping for a ducal son-in-law and was wantonly blind to the danger in which her daughter stood.

'You are very silent, Prue,' the Duke remarked as they drove through the dark streets where oil lamps only occasionally shed a pool of light.

'I find nothing to say to you.'

'Yet I have much I wish to say to you, Prue.' He bent forward to look into her face. 'Will you not hear me?'

Suddenly her control snapped. She turned to meet his intent eyes, her own blazing.

'Do you wish to tell me of your wager with Lord Barony?' Anger and pain drove her on, the words tumbling out in a furious spate. 'The wager that all London smiles at? Is it nothing to you that a woman's reputation is put at risk? Do you hate me so much you must ruin me? Is your vanity so great that you think you—'

His hand was on her arm, gripping so tightly that it hurt, making her pause.

'What folly is this?' he demanded harshly. 'What have you heard? What wager do I make? Come, I'll have the truth!'

'You shall have it, sir.' She began to tremble. 'It is brought to my notice that you . . . you have wagered with my Lord Barony you will—will prevail with me!' She sank back against the cushions, staring blindly out of the window as hot tears blurred her vision.

In the silence that followed her words she heard the uneven pounding of her heart and the sudden, swift intake of breath of the man beside her whose hand still gripped her. When at last he spoke, she shrank from the bitter cruelty edging his voice.

'So I wager my success with an ill-begotten debauchee? I make your name a peg on which to hang rumour, scandal, evil? 'Fore God, you make me out a truly noble character! Well, you shall not be disappointed, my dear.'

Before she could move, he had caught her in his arms and his mouth was on hers, kissing her with cruel passion, bruising her tender lips while his arms crushed her against his hard body. She had no strength to resist. Her anger, hurt and fear dissolved in a rush of feeling that burned her like a flame. She was alive to passion, responding, caught in a whirlwind of feeling she had never known, never suspected. Her arms were around him, her mouth answered his. She was drowning in a fierce ecstasy that was edged with pain.

Abruptly he let her go. In the darkness of the coach she could not see his face, but she could hear his quick, uneven breathing.

'So you are no ice-maiden,' he said bitterly. 'You cannot make yourself hate me; but you believe I am capable of making your name a byword with all the foolish world!'

'I . . . I was told . . .' She could not go on.

'Aye, you were told—and you believed! You have had much reason to mistrust me, Prue, to harden your heart against me, but tonight I . . . Now, I see you would believe any evil of me!'

The cold anger in his voice was like a sword in her heart. 'Very well, I shall not trouble you again! 'Fore God in heaven, I swear I shall wait for you to come to me!'

The coach had stopped. Hardly knowing what she did, Prue let the footman hand her down the steps and escort her to the door of the house. James opened it and she stepped inside without a backward glance, and stood listening to the sounds of fading hoofbeats and the rattle of wheels upon cobbles.

'The family have retired, Mistress Prue,' James said, looking at her a little anxiously. 'You seem—agitated. Is there aught I can do?'

'Thank you James, no.' She went up the stairs slowly. In

her room, she dismissed a sleepy Mollie and sank down upon the bed and burst into a storm of weeping.

At first all thought was chaotic, but as her tears slowly ceased, she raised her head and tried to think more clearly. Had Elise indeed been mistaken? Surely she would never have invented such a story even in a fit of jealousy? Elise was selfish, flighty, quick-tempered and spoilt, but not wicked, not subtle enough to work out such a plan to be rid of a rival. Besides, Elise could not be certain of John's love for her friend, and she was very sure of her own powers to enchant. Elise had heard something, some spiteful gossip about the Duke's attention to the eldest Miss Angel. His reputation was such that any notice paid to one so far beneath him in rank must arouse ill-natured speculation.

'And I was ready to believe it of him,' Prue thought, pressing her hands against her throbbing temples.

He had been angry, bitterly angry that she had believed it! He was finished with her; he would never see her again! He would forget her!

'And I shall never forget him!' Her heart was telling her the truth at last. 'Because I love him most deeply . . . and I always shall, alas!'

# CHAPTER NINETEEN

PRUE awoke from a heavy sleep to hear her door being opened softly.

'La, sister, I thought you'd never waken,' Cassie said, coming into the room. She pulled back the curtains, letting in a flood of bright sunshine. 'See, 'tis past noon. Mama is still abed, she complains of a chill brought by the night air, but it is more likely she drank champagne, which don't agree with her.'

She came over to the bed. 'Did you like the evening, Prue? I thought you looked unwell at times, and now you have black shadows under your eyes.' She dropped on to the bed with her eyes fixed on Prue's pale face. 'Were you greatly vexed at Mama's accepting the Duke's offer to bring you home? I tried to prevent her being so eager, but she would have it, and I still have a bruise where she nipped me.'

'I was not pleased,' Prue told her, sitting up and shaking back her dark curls. Her cap had fallen off during her restless tossing through the night. 'It was vastly unwise of Mama, she should not have done such a thing.'

'Indeed, Mrs Courtney looked quite amazed, since there was room for you with us. But Mama is for ever taken with the notion that you'll catch the Duke for a husband.'

Prue looked down at her arm where a faint bruise showed. It was where the Duke's hand had gripped her last night, a night that would live for ever in her heart.

'Shall I bring you some coffee?' Cassie asked. 'Or shall Lizzie bring you one of her cordials?'

Prue shook her head as she slipped out of bed. 'I want nothing, thank you. Cassie,' she looked up to meet her sister's eyes, 'I am leaving for Northumberland as soon as I may. I am . . . weary of London and its society. I prefer to return to Papa, he misses me, I know.'

Cassie was silent for some minutes. At last she nodded and rose.

'I'll not ask questions, sister. You have always been one to know your mind and you have good reason, I expect. Mama will be in a fine fret, but it will be nothing so unusual.' She smiled ruefully. ''Twould seem we were brought here for no purpose—well, not *her* purpose. First Selina and now you, and it will not be long before I am in the same way of setting her in sad disappointment, for I mean to marry Harry, you know.'

Lady Angel did not rise from her bed until late afternoon when she settled herself, with cordial, lavender water and lozenges, on the sofa and let Lizzie tuck a rug around her.

'The damp night air has ever affected me,' she complained to her daughters.

'Then you were vastly unwise to choose to attend a night entertainment on the river, were you not?' Cassie asked, and was told to hold her tongue if she had nothing better to do but tease her suffering mother.

Prue saw that there would be no use in attempting to discuss anything with her mother, and endured an evening of reminiscences of all the nobility who had graciously taken notice of their party, and how envious her friend Dorcas had been.

Presently Prue slipped away to the library and sat down to write to her father, giving him notice of her intention to return home. She gave no reason, knowing her father would not press for one. A longing to be gone, to leave the city that had brought her such bitter heartache, came to her as she wrote. In her northern home she would find the peace and quiet she needed. She summoned a footman and sent him out to post the letter.

She slept little that night. Frightening pictures rose before her, always dominated by the same tall, elegant figure of the man she loved and whose love—if indeed he did love her— she could never accept. She remembered the steely anger in his eyes and the grim set of his jaw when he said: 'So you are no ice-maiden! You cannot make yourself hate me!' She had given herself away, and he knew she loved him ... and he had spurned her when he knew she believed ill of him.

The thought came abruptly: Elise! She must see Elise and discover more.

Her chance came next morning, when she and Cassie drove with Lady Angel to the Mall and there left their mother and walked along the tree-lined path and she saw Elise coming towards her.

'Elise, I am glad we are met,' she said, catching her friend's hand. 'I must speak with you, it is important.'

Elise gave her a quick glance and frowned faintly. 'I am to meet Mama and John at the gate.'

'I will walk with you. Cassie has met Harry, and will be quite agreeable to being left alone with him.'

As soon as they were out of earshot of the others, Prue drew Elise into a side path where they were alone.

'Elise, you must tell me more of where and how you heard this story of your cousin and Lord Barony, for I am persuaded you have been greatly misled in the matter.' She watched Elise's mobile little face and saw the quick look of dismay across it.

'But already I tell you! It was Lord Barony's sister who tells me. Her brother says he and Charles have a wager—'

'I am convinced it is untrue!'

'You have not spoken of it to Charles?' There was no mistaking the alarm in Elise's eyes. 'Oh, how *could* you be so indelicate! To bring yourself to speak . . . Did you say it was I who told you?'

'No, but I am certain it is not true, and you must at once deny this wicked rumour, Elise, for my sake—and his.'

Elise shrugged and pursed her lips. 'Oh, la, it is possible Barony's sister makes too much of the matter . . . or I somewhat misunderstood her. But there is no smoke unless there is fire, you know, and I was perfectly right to warn you against Charles. Just to be seen with him will cause people to whisper—and I could not bear your reputation to be injured. I thought only of you, you know.'

Suddenly she put her hands to her eyes and said in a muffled voice: 'Oh sweet Prue, do not look at me so coldly! If I was mistaken, it is because I am in such a misery of fear and distress that I do not know what I do! I am the most *miserable* of women, Prue!'

'Why, what has happened?' Prue asked in swift sympathy as she saw Elise's face crumple.

'I—I cannot tell you, no, not yet! But I think I am in much danger and I am so afraid! Oh, Prue,' she grasped Prue's hand, 'if I ever should send for you, if I implored you to come and aid me, would you come?'

'But of course, Elise. But what is this trouble? Cannot you tell your mother?'

'Oh, no, *no*! She must never know, never! But *you* can help me! *Promise* you will come if I should ever send for you!'

'Very well, I promise,' Prue agreed. 'But I cannot imagine what——'

'Do not speak of it! I am positively ill with worry! Perhaps it is why I listen to wicked gossip about Charles.'

She turned and walked stiffly away. Prue watched her go, then slowly retraced her steps and caught up with Cassie and Harry.

. . . . . .

That afternoon Prue sought her mother and told her she wished to return to Northumberland. Lady Angel stared at her for a full minute, her mouth open. At last she exclaimed, 'Go *home*? Have you lost your wits? When we are engaged to attend the Richmond rout—and an evening at Ranelagh with——'

'I have lost all interest in the fashionable world, Mama. I wish to leave London. I shall travel post and take Mollie with me——'

'You shall do no such thing!' An angry red mottled Lady Angel's cheeks. 'I have worn myself out to bring you in the way of polite society, you and your sisters! Selina has showed little gratitude, although. . . . But that you should treat me in such a wicked manner . . .'

'I am grateful, Mama, for all you have done,' Prue said quietly but with a firmness that alarmed her mother. 'I am sorry I disappoint you, but I do not remain in London. I have written to Papa to expect me shortly.'

'Oh, your father will support you in any naughtiness,' her mother burst out, 'he has always spoiled you, and I have told him so! Am I to be left alone, then?'

'You will have Cassie and your many friends. And the season will soon be over.'

Her mother's eyes narrowed suddenly. 'Prue, has the Duke . . . Was he attentive to you after the river party? 'Twas unfortunate, no doubt, that we had no room in any of our carriages and I had to accept his offer.'

'Vastly unfortunate,' Prue said tensely, 'because the Duke did *not* invite me to become his duchess! The Duke of Carlington does not marry beneath his rank, as I have already promised you.'

'But he has shown you such favour. . . . Do not tell me he was but flirting with you?'

'I fear I can tell you nothing,' Prue moved resolutely towards the door, 'except that I shall arrange to return to the north as soon as possible.'

To her relief, her mother did not press the matter. Something in Prue's manner told her it would be useless to protest, and she consoled herself by complaining bitterly to Cassie and making Lizzie's life a misery for several days.

Cassie came to Prue and found her sorting out clothes for the journey.

'I think 'tis well you're going,' she said bluntly, 'you look pale, and I know you are not happy. I shall see that Mama is kept busy with parties and cards, and 'twill not be long before we too shall leave for home.' She watched Prue fold a night-robe. 'Prue, will you allow Harry to accompany you?' Prue looked up in surprise and saw colour rise in Cassie's cheeks. 'He wishes to see Papa, and you will know why. He asks if he may travel with you and look after you.'

Prue agreed at once. To have a man like Harry with her would make the long journey vastly more agreeable and comfortable.

'The Courtneys are come,' Cassie told her, 'and Hester asks for you.'

'Pray ask her to come to me here,' Prue said, 'I am not in the mood for a social gathering, I fear.'

When Hester came into the bedroom she stood staring at the valises, hat-boxes and piles of clothes on the bed.

'Prue, what is this? Do you go on a visit?'

'I have decided to leave London.' Prue went to her friend and put her arm around her shoulders. 'I regret nothing but leaving Cassie and you. I . . . have reason to wish to return home.'

Hester said nothing for a moment, while her eyes searched Prue's face. At last she said,

'Forgive my asking if it is painful to you, dearest Prue, but has this anything to do with the Duke of Carlington?'

A great longing to confide in her friend swept over Prue. Her family must never know the truth, but Hester was to be trusted. Haltingly at first, then in a rush of painful confession, she told of her rejection of the Duke's offer to make her his mistress, and the disaster of her attachment to him, and her resolve to flee from London and all chance of ever meeting him again.

'Oh, Prue my dear, how greatly you have suffered!' Hester cried warmly. 'I guessed there was something . . . The Duke showed you unusual attention. How evil men have grown in modern society!'

'He is not evil,' Prue said unhappily, 'he behaves as all men in his position, wealthy, powerful, of highest birth, will behave. It is not possible that he should marry anyone beneath him in rank. There are women who would—would——'

'Would accept his offer with eagerness, yes, it is so,' Hester sighed. 'You are wise to leave, but I shall sadly miss you. You know you can trust me never to speak of this.'

Prue, too, felt sadness at parting from a friend she cherished. They bade each other farewell, and Hester went down to join her mother in the drawing-room.

Harry proved invaluable. Lady Angel refused to do anything to help, and preserved a sulky silence towards Prue. But Harry arranged coach tickets for them all, and discovered the time of starting and pauses en route. Mollie was excited at the prospect of a journey, and packed and sorted clothes with Prue. But one gown, a rose satin with a woven pattern in gold, was left out, as Lady Angel had insisted on Prue's accompanying her and Cassie to the Richmond rout, and rather than anger her mother further, Prue had agreed.

Her heart was not in tune with the preparations for the rout. The Duke, John had mentioned, would not be there. Even so, all charm in gaieties of the modish world had died for her, and she paid little heed how her hair was dressed or what jewels she wore. She prayed that the evening would pass as swiftly as possible and that it would be her last appearance in society.

John had insisted on escorting them to the rout and Prue had a twinge of uneasiness, feeling that his place should be with Madame de la Fournes and her daughter. It would not please Elise, who already had some private trouble to distress her. Had the pretty butterfly embroiled herself with someone unsuitable? Had she behaved with rashness and was regretting it? Had she, who loved pretty clothes and jewels, got into debt and was afraid to tell her mother?

Remembering Elise's unhappy confession of fear, Prue wished she could be of help, although it was unlikely now she was to leave London. She had not seen Elise to tell her of her imminent departure; no doubt there would be opportunity to tell her at the rout.

The brilliant parade of the fashionable world disporting itself amid scenes of beauty and luxury did nothing to raise Prue's spirits. There was a heaviness in her heart that nothing could allay. She danced, smiled and conversed mechanically, and when at last she found herself alone, she slipped out of the room and into a long conservatory filled with palms and ferns and banks of exotic blooms. Here it was cool, and she could be alone with her thoughts. She dropped into a seat hidden by a stand of ferns—and was dismayed to hear footsteps, and see John standing before her.

'I saw you leave the room,' he said quickly and a little breathlessly, 'and I feared you felt faint.'

'Oh no,' she assured him, touched by his anxiety. 'It was so hot, and it is pleasantly cool here. But you must not be taken from the dancing. I am perfectly well here. There are many beauties awaiting to partner you.'

'And I want none of them!' he burst out, sinking to his knee before her. 'Prue my dearest, most angelic and lovely Prue, you cannot be unaware of my adoration for you, my growing passion which I can no longer hide, my devotion! Since I first saw you my heart has been yours!'

'Oh, pray hush! Do not continue,' she begged him in distress. 'Dear John, I have always valued your friendship and been grateful for your kindness to my family, but—I cannot offer you more than this.'

'I will wait,' he caught her hand, his face eager with longing, 'for ever, if I must! There is no other woman in the world who can ever mean anything to me! Let me worship you, and perhaps one day your heart——'

He broke off as Prue turned her head sharply, hearing a sound. The screen of ferns was thick, but surely she had heard a step . . . and was there not a glimmer of yellow satin and a swift rustle of skirts as the wearer moved away?

'John,' she spoke kindly, but there was something in her voice that drained the hope from his face, 'I shall ever treasure your love and feel honoured, but I cannot, ever, return it. It saddens me greatly that I have hurt you, but in time you will forget me.'

'Never, I swear it!' he declared passionately. 'Prue, is this truly your last word?'

'Yes, John,' she said, caught in sadness.

He rose and stood looking at her, his face pale and set. Then he raised her hand to his lips, and left her.

'Oh, why could I not love him?' she thought wearily. 'He most truly loves me and is good and kind.'

Her heart answered her: 'Because you love another man.'

She sat for a while, oppressed by a strange feeling of shadows gathering around her, darkening her thoughts and presaging danger. But she would be gone in a few days' time, surely no danger could touch her before then!

She returned to the ballroom, hoping to find her mother ready to leave. The crowds were thinning and Cassie was looking bored and restless as she came up.

'Oh lord, 'tis a dull affair if Harry does not attend,' she remarked, stifling a yawn. 'Let us persuade Mama to leave. I vow my eyes are perfectly tired by these garish gowns—and the most garish of them all is your little friend, Mademoiselle Elise, who resembles nothing so much as a brimstone butterfly in her yellow gown and topaz ornaments.'

Prue caught her breath, but before she could speak, a brilliant splash of colour detached itself from the throng and darted over to them.

'Dearest Prue!' Elise's voice was a shade too high. 'I have not had time to speak with you in this stupid crush! So you still remain in London? I thought——'

'La, why should she leave before the season ends?' Cassie broke in, eyeing Elise coolly. ''Tis the time packed with most gaiety, I'm told. I have persuaded her to keep me company.'

Before Prue could protest, Madame de la Fournes called her daughter peremptorily to her side and Elise, after a swift glance at Prue, hastened to join her.

'Cassie, what is your purpose in pretending I am to stay in London?' Prue demanded. 'You know perfectly well I shall leave.'

'I know perfectly well that that little puss wishes you out of the way of John, and I delight to keep her guessing. It will give her something to worry about.'

Prue's distress increased as she watched the de la Fournes party leave. There had been other yellow gowns, and it was of course possible it had not been Elise behind the screen of ferns when John had declared his passion. She hoped fervently that it had not. If Elise was truly in love with John she would be hurt and unhappy.

She was grateful for John's absence when it was time to depart. Lady Angel remarked upon it, but Cassie, after a quick glance at her sister's face, began to discuss the guests and their gowns, both subjects sure of catching her mother's attention.

'I did not observe Dorcas or her daughters,' Lady Angel remarked with some satisfaction. 'It is possible that they are not really in the first rank of the tonnish world. But at least she has two obedient and satisfactory children,' she cast an irritated glance at Cassie and Prue, 'who do not selfishly remove themselves from their mother's side or pretend unsuitable attachments.'

'I do *not* pretend,' Cassie said obstinately.

Prue remained silent. Today was Wednesday. On Saturday she would be on her way home under the care of Harry. London would be left behind but not, alas, memories.

On a last shopping trip next day she met the Misses Beauford who expressed amazement at her voluntarily forgoing draining the last drop of entertainment from the London season.

'But perhaps your visit has proved a disappointment to you,' Caro suggested, smiling slyly.

Her sister shook her head. 'Prue has been a success, has it not been said she is one of the season's beauties? She could have all the beaux she wanted.'

'But perhaps she could not get the one she wanted,' Caro sniggered.

Minnie frowned. 'Tush, Caro, how you love to scratch. Pay her no heed, Prue, she is in a muffish mood because her fiancé forgets her birthday. I shall miss your company, Prue.'

Prue was alone next evening when the message came. Lady Angel and Cassie had gone to play cards with friends, and Mollie and Lizzie had been given the evening off. The footman brought her the letter and said that a coach was at the door.

Startled, Prue opened the letter and read: 'Oh most dear and true friend, you promised to come to me if I shall need you! I am in most grave and terrible trouble and implore you to come to me *at once*! I need your help! Do not fail me, dear Prue, but come without delay. Your unhappy and distracted Elise.'

Prue sprang to her feet. 'Oh, heavens, what has the poor girl put herself into? Pray the Lord I may be able to help her!'

She ran to her room, found her pelisse and hurried to the front door, telling the footman to explain she had gone to visit a friend, should her mother return before she did.

The coach was a hired one, somewhat old and shabby, but Prue was too perturbed to take much notice of it or the route it took through the darkening streets. Her thoughts were all on Elise, and what could have occurred for her to have sent such an impassioned appeal for help.

However, after a time she began to wonder how much longer it would take her to reach her friend. The coach had left the main thoroughfare and was driving along what appeared to be a lonely road without lights or buildings on it. She wondered if Elise had tried to run away, and had taken fright and was waiting to be rescued at some remote spot, and the thought became a certainty when the coach rolled into a yard and stopped before a small, dismal-looking inn with a cracked sign swinging in the wind.

Prue stepped out, telling the coachman to wait, and approached the inn entrance. As she stepped inside the door she was startled to hear the rumble of wheels on cobbles and turning, saw the coach disappearing into the darkness. For a moment she hesitated, aware of sudden uneasiness, then a frowzy woman addressed her, saying that her friend awaited her in an upper room, and pointed up the narrow stairs before shuffling back to the tap room.

Prue gathered her pelisse around her and started up the stairs, thinking that Elise, with her usual rashness, had chosen an unsavoury place for a meeting. A door ahead of her was slightly ajar and she caught the gleam of candlelight and heard movement within.

She hurried into the room, shutting the door behind her.

'You see,' she said quickly, 'I have come to you. . . .'

She broke off with a gasp as she saw the figure standing by the window turn to look at her. A tall, broad-shouldered figure in silver-grey. His Grace the Duke of Carlington.

# CHAPTER TWENTY

FOR a moment shock held Prue frozen. Her eyes *must* deceive her! It could not be the man she had sworn never to meet again! Where was Elise? Had she also summoned her cousin to help her? What had happened to her?

'Prue!' In a few strides he was before her, gripping her hands in his strong clasp. In the light of the flickering candle she could not see his face clearly. 'At last you have come to me! When I declared you would come, I did not dare to think . . . I hardly hoped you would come!'

She dragged her hands away, shrinking back. 'You are mistaken! I came in answer to a message from . . .'

Suddenly it burst upon her. Elise *had* overheard John's declaration of love in the conservatory that night, and blind jealousy had driven her to this! Convinced that Prue did not mean to heed her warning and leave London, and aware that John would look at no other woman while Prue was near, she had planned and laid this plot to lure her 'sweet friend' into the power of the Perfidious Devil, trusting in his power to overcome her resistance. Even if this did not succeed, Prue's reputation would be ruined, for she knew that Elise would make it known she had met the Duke at a lonely inn and on her own.

'Do not pretend to me, Prue,' the Duke said sternly, his eyes on her white face. 'I received your message and came as you bade me. Though why you chose this ramshackle place . . .'

'My message?' She put a trembling hand to her face. 'I sent

you no message! You are most gravely mistaken if you think I wished a meeting. It is a plot to ruin me! I shall leave this instant!'

'No, Prue, you shall not!' He had her in his arms, a trembling prisoner. 'I care not how or why you are here! I have had no rest, no quiet of mind since you accused me of evil and I left you. You fill my life, I cannot, no matter how I try, forget you! And now I know you love me I shall never let you go!'

As he bent his head to kiss her, she was seized with a panic so strong that she managed to tear herself away and pull the door behind her open. She fled down the stairs as he cried,

'Prue . . . Come back! You must listen to me! I tried to tell you in the coach that night . . .'

But she was racing down the steep stairs, her mind shut to all but the need to escape before she surrendered to him, before her resistance broke down and carried her on to disaster. She heard his step on the stairs behind her as she ran to the inn door.

Suddenly her way was barred and a thick voice said, 'Nay, my pretty wench, not so fast I pray. Come, I'll stand ye a drink of brandy and we'll have rare sport! I've a room upstairs.'

He was a foppish, thick-set man, his face flushed with wine and a lecherous smile on his loose mouth as he grabbed at her.

'Let me go!' she cried.

'Never! You're mine this night, sweetheart!' He stooped to pick her up. She cried out, and felt his arms slacken as he was dragged back by a merciless hand on his collar.

'Damn you, Carlington, are you foxed? 'Tis but a wench I've a mind to tumble . . .'

Prue saw the Duke strike and the man stumble and fall, cursing, before she escaped into the darkness of the stable yard where a small, elegant chaise stood ready to depart. The coachman had gathered up the reins and a gentleman was about to enter as she ran up. He turned and the lantern lit his face and with a sob of thankfulness she clutched his arm, gasping out,

'Mr Unwin! Oh, I pray and beg you will take me in your chaise. . . . At once! Oh, *hurry*!'

''Fore God, 'tis Mistress Prue Angel!' He was staring, his plump face for once startled out of its smug solemnity. He glanced nervously at the inn from whence came angry shouts. 'What can bring you here at this time——'

'Do not wait!' She sprang past him and into the chaise. He cast another glance behind him, and seeing figures coming from the inn, followed her hastily, calling to his driver to whip up the horses. In a minute they were bowling along the dark road and Prue, crouching in her corner, was trying to recover her breath and bring her mind into some order to deal with the situation.

Luckily for her, Mr Richard Unwin, Minnie Beauford's promised husband, was also recovering from a medley of emotions, and as the proceeding took him longer than it did Prue, she was ready before he was.

'You are astonished to see me in such a set-up,' she said shakily, 'Oh, sir! I have been through an experience! A terrible experience!'

'I am indeed much amazed, Mistress Prue. What can have happened?'

'I set out to visit a friend, and took a hackney,' she told him, inventing wildly and praying he would take it as truth, 'and we were—were set upon by a highwayman who, finding I had neither jewels nor money, carried me off to that dreadful inn! While he drank, I escaped. God knows what might have happened if you had not been there! I thank you most heartily, sir, for being my saviour!'

For a moment he sat staring at her, murmuring: 'Lord bless me! Such villainy . . . a helpless gentlewoman kidnapped . . . a crime of the first water! We must alert the constables ... report the outrage!'

She leaned forward quickly. 'Oh pray, Mr Unwin, do no such thing! The wretch will have flown now he finds I have escaped. He—he was masked, so I do not know how he looks—and the inn folk will not betray him, for sure!'

'But, the law....'

'The law will not restore my reputation, sir, if tonight's work be known.' She looked at him earnestly. 'You know society and its love of scandal, and how much can be made of so little. I shall be accused of seeking some assignation, or ...' She faltered for a second, seeking words to convince him. 'A woman's virtue has but to have a breath of suspicion cast on it to be ruined for ever. Promise me you will speak of tonight's work to no one, *no* one, I beg of you!'

Her hood had fallen back and her curls clung in soft disorder about her face. A delicate colour showed in her cheeks and her great dark eyes were on his, beseeching him. No gallant man—and Richard Unwin, stodgy and prosy as he was, was a gallant and kindly man—could withstand that appeal.

'Very well, Mistress Prue. Since you ask it of me, I give you my promise. But your family——'

'I can trust them.' She sank back, suddenly weak and trembling, and heard Richard saying,

'I have a flask ... A sip of brandy, Miss Prue—I insist.'

She accepted it, and felt the fiery spirit bring some warmth to her chilled body. The light chaise travelled faster than the hackney had done, and already they were entering the suburbs of the city. A lassitude had her in its grip and her thoughts were becoming clouded. But one thought stood out: tomorrow she would leave this great city, to which she had come with such high hopes, for ever.

Richard handed her from the chaise when it stopped before the house and his eyes were troubled as he asked, 'You are perfectly sure you will be all right, Mistress Prue? It has been a terrible experience for you. When I think of what might have happened had I not stopped at that inn. . . .'

'Do not think of it,' she murmured, touched by his concern. 'I shall not. Farewell, Mr Unwin.' She put her hand on his for a second and added, smiling wistfully, 'You know, sir, I think Minnie is a vastly lucky girl!'

James opened the door and looked at her reproachfully. 'Mistress Prue! Her ladyship has quite fretted herself into a state about you! Leaving no message and——'

'I visited a friend,' she said quickly, 'and—and the hackney broke down and we were delayed. I shall go to Lady Angel at once.'

Luckily her mother was too sleepy to do more than scold her for a thoughtless, reckless creature to drive alone in a hackney and added, as Prue slipped from the room, that it was as well, perhaps, she was to return to country life and keep herself out of mischief.

Mollie exclaimed at Prue's exhausted appearance. 'Oh, fie, Miss Prue! And you have a journey on the morrow and need rest!'

'I shall be all right, Mollie. Do you take yourself off to your bed.'

But Mollie refused to leave until she had seen her mistress tucked up in bed with a drink of hot milk and wine. She lingered at the door, looking anxious. 'Is there aught else you need, mistress? You're that pale . . . and your eyes so weary.'

'Leave me, Mollie, I shall do very well. We must be busy tomorrow.'

Once the girl had gone, memory had Prue in its cruel grip. That Elise could have treated her so vilely! That her jealousy had burned so hot within her that it left no room for pity or friendship. Had jealousy always lain hidden beneath a show of love? It was clear, now, that she had invented the story of the wager in the hope it would drive Prue from London and leave John to be wooed by her wiles. To be rid of Prue she had risked all. She knew the Duke's reputation and his feelings towards Prue, and she may have guessed that Prue was afraid of her own heart and hoped she would surrender under attack; and that John, and the modish world, would know and condemn.

Prue put her hand to her throbbing head. 'Well, she will have her wish. I shall never return to London.'

Early next morning, while Mollie was seeing to the last of the packing, Prue went to the library, and was finishing a letter of farewell to Hester when she heard a commotion in the hall. She rose to her feet as the door opened and James, looking somewhat flustered, announced, 'Lady Anne Bouchier.'

Lady Anne, an imposing figure in a grey sack gown and Indian shawl, advanced upon the startled Prue. She was looking distraught and her rouge stood out on her blanched face.

'I have come myself to beg you will return with me, Mistress Angel! He asks for you continually, and will not settle . . . The surgeon says that the wound cannot heal unless he rests. Fever has set in!'

Prue started forward, her hands clasped to her breast, her eyes wide with horror.

'Wounded? The Duke? How? Why?'

'A duel.' Lady Anne's mouth quivered. 'This morning, in the park. I know not what madness caused it. Charles was the better swordsman, but there was dew upon the grass and his foot slipped. He asks for you, and you must come! I shall not return without you!'

For a second the room rocked about Prue and she caught at the back of a chair to prevent herself falling. He was hurt, perhaps badly, perhaps fatally. The man she loved lay sorely wounded, calling for her!

'I will come,' she whispered, and hastened into the hall, calling the footman to send Mollie to her. When Mollie came, wide-eyed, she said: 'Tell Lady Angel that I am gone with Lady Anne Bouchier to the Duke of Carlington's residence.'

They drove in silence. Prue dared not ask how badly the Duke was wounded, fearing the answer. They found the Duke's house in turmoil. Prue followed Lady Anne up the great flight of stairs and into an anteroom where a valet, major-domo and two servants waited silently.

'The surgeon is with His Grace,' the major-domo whispered to Lady Anne, his eyes going curiously to Prue, pale and trembling behind her. 'His Grace has been let blood twice.'

A door opened and John Hillier came out. He started on seeing Prue, then addressed himself to Lady Anne, saying in a low voice, 'The fever is rising, I fear, and he is very restless and in pain.'

Prue stepped forward. 'Take me to him,' she said quietly.

John hesitated, then at a nod from Lady Anne, he bowed and opened the door for Prue to pass through.

For a moment she could see little. The curtains had been drawn and the room seemed full of shadows, the only light coming from two lamps near the bed. She paused, shaken by the rush of emotion that overwhelmed her, then she went forward softly and stood looking down at the man she had run away from last night, the man she had meant never to see again, the man who had her heart for ever.

He was very pale, and sweat stood out on his forehead and chin and he breathed unevenly. His hair, dank with sweat, clung to his head and his eyes were shut. Looking at him, Prue felt her blood turn to ice. Suddenly he opened his eyes, those grey eyes that had so often and arrogantly met hers, and he whispered, so low that she had to stoop to hear, 'Prue . . . you have come. . . . Do not . . . leave me . . . again.'

She sank upon her knees, heedless of the surgeon silently watching them.

'I am here, Charles, and I shall not leave you! You must

rest, you must recover—for my sake.'

A faint smile touched his mouth, the mouth she had once thought cruel.

'For *your* sake? Faith, death shall . . . not take me now!'

She watched his eyes close and heard the little sigh of contentment. The surgeon moved closer to the bed.

'You have calmed him, madam. It is what he needs.'

She looked up fearfully into his face. 'Is he . . . is he badly hurt, sir?'

'The wound is not deep, but fever has him in its grip. However, he is strong and now he appears tranquil. If you will stay. . . .'

She said steadily: 'I shall stay.'

In the hours that followed she did not leave his side. He moaned sometimes, seeming restless, and she would place her hand on his burning forehead and speak softly, and he would stare at her, smile and relax.

Suddenly she became aware of Lady Anne stooping over her.

'You must rest, my child. Charles sleeps more calmly, and the surgeon says that you may safely leave him for a time. Come, you must eat something.'

Under Lady Anne's insistence Prue managed to swallow some food and drink a glass of Madeira, but all her thoughts were with the sick man.

'Is it known, Lady Anne, how the duel came about?' she ventured to ask, and saw Lady Anne's face tighten for a second.

''Twas some brawl in a low tavern last night, I fear. Charles struck Lord Barony, who demanded satisfaction. I do not even know the cause of the affair.'

Prue was silent. She knew the cause, and the knowledge was deeply painful and yet glorious. He had fought for her honour, because she had been assaulted, and he had been struck down. She rose swiftly saying, 'I must go to him.'

His eyes were bright with fever when she approached the bed, and he reached out to catch her hand as he whispered painfully,

'Prue, will you ever . . . forgive me? Can you forgive the wrong I would have done you?'

'Hush,' she murmured, 'you must try to rest.'

'I cannot rest! You will never know . . . how deeply I have hated myself, how bitterly I regret . . . how I have come to realise my blind arrogance. . . .'

'Hush,' she said again, but he moved his head restlessly.

'I must speak. That evening in the coach I had planned . . . Last night I wanted to . . . but you ran away from me!' His breath came quickly through his dry lips. 'I thought I had lost you! I thought you had come to me, but you left me before I could ask you!'

She put her hand on his hot forehead and looked deep into his eyes.

'I will do whatever you ask of me, my dearest one,' she said softly. 'I love you, and I am yours for ever.'

'You will marry me—and forgive? If . . . you refuse . . . I shall not wish to live, Prue.'

She saw the pleading in his eyes and tears rose in her own as she whispered: 'Oh Charles, my dear heart, I promise—if indeed it is your wish!'

He raised her hand to his lips, smiled and closed his eyes, and was sleeping peacefully when the surgeon entered.

'I vow you have saved me, sister,' Cassie remarked as she sat with Prue in the morning room some weeks later. 'Mama is in such a swim of joy that Papa's letter permitting Harry to offer for me caused nothing greater than a lifted eyebrow. I am persuaded her dear friend Dorcas Beauford leaves town solely because she is in the fidgets with all Mama's raptures!'

She leaned back, playing with her embroidery. 'The end of

the season is vastly dull, and most of our friends are gone. The Courtneys return to Devonshire, and John Hillier takes his broken heart to Italy. However, Papa and Harry will be with us soon.' She sighed rapturously.

Prue was not listening to her. Her ears strained to hear the sound of carriage wheels and swift, impatient steps in the hall. Suddenly she lifted her head, her eyes glowing.

Cassie laughed and got up. 'I leave you to your declared lover; am I not a model sister?' She ran from the room as Charles entered.

'Charles!' Prue ran into his arms, her heart lifting joyfully as she slipped her arms around his neck. He kissed her, with tenderness, longing and passion, until she cried for mercy.

Later, when they were sitting in the deep window seat, she said, 'Charles, it is true I did not send that message asking you to meet me at the inn. Someone. . . .' she hesitated, '. . . was playing a trick on both of us.'

She saw his face darken. 'And I know well who played it—and why. Elise confessed when she thought I was about to expire. Her mother has taken her back to France, much to poor John's relief. She is a spiteful little cat, and you did ill to trust her, my sweet. Yet I sometimes think if we had not met at the inn that night——'

'And you had not struck Lord Barony. . . .'

'And you had not thought it your duty, being the cause of my wound, to save my life by agreeing to marry me——' He pulled her close to him, smiling down into her eyes. 'A poor devil such as I does not deserve an angel!'

Laughter lit her dancing eyes. 'Faith, I am not sure you have one, Charles—except in name!'

''Twill serve. Come, kiss me, sweet angel.'

'Oh most certainly, my lord Devil!' she murmured, and raised her face to meet his kiss.

# Masquerade
Historical Romances

# Intrigue excitement romance

Don't miss
August's
other enthralling Historical Romance title

**MEETING AT SCUTARI**
*by Belinda Grey*

The boring round of trivial politeness endured by all women in Victorian society has not prepared Jessica Linton for the devastating charm of Prince Paul Varinsky. How can she have fallen in love with so totally unsuitable a man? Not only is he married – and Jessica is unwilling to risk a scandal – but he is Russian, England's foe in the war brewing in Turkey. Desperate to blot him from her mind, Jessica embarks for Scutari in the Crimea as one of Florence Nightingale's staff, dedicated to saving lives in the primitive conditions there. A chance encounter reunites her with the one man she is trying to forget – an enemy now both of her country and her patriotic heart . . .

You can obtain this title today from your local paperback retailer

# Masquerade
## Historical Romances

**CROMWELL'S CAPTAIN**
*by Anne Madden*

Why should Cathie Gifford, who came of a staunchly Royalist family, feel compelled to tend the wounded Roundhead captain? And why should a man like Piers Denham, who had betrayed his own kind by fighting for Parliament, be able to shake her loyalty to the King?

**HOUSE OF SATAN**
*by Gina Veronese*

Count Anton von Arnheim's Viennese mansion was notorious, even in the pleasure-loving society of 1785. And into it came Eloise, the Count's innocent and beautiful ward. How long could she go on living happily in the House of Satan?

Look out for these titles in your local paperback shop from
12th September 1980